LOAVES & WISHES

ELIZABETH MADDREY

For my Family

R uth Baxter dropped her suitcase on the gleaming dark wood floors and pushed the front door closed before sagging against it. Home? What had Naomi been thinking? From somewhere in the depths of Ruth's enormous purse, her cell rang. She dug around, her fingers closing around the device just as it stopped. She dragged it out and glanced at the screen. Jonah. Of course it was Jonah. And her other two brothers were probably in the room with him. When their parents died more than ten years ago, the four of them had become inseparable. Until now. The phone chimed with a request for a video chat.

Stifling a groan, she swiped across the screen and tapped accept. "Hey. I just got here."

Jonah grinned and stepped backwards. The faces of Malachi and Micah joined his in the camera's eye. "And? How's your inheritance?"

Ruth flipped the phone around so they could see the foyer with its gleaming antiques. "This is as far as I've made it."

"Not really your style, is it?" That was Micah.

Ruth flipped the phone around and shrugged. "No. But then,

I'm having a hard time seeing Naomi choose these, either. Neither of us ever loved all things Victoriana. Maybe it suits the clientele? Or maybe it's an opportunity to start over, put my own mark on things."

"That's my sister. Always the optimist." Jonah made a goofy face.

"Have to be, with you three around. No pithy comments, Malachi?" Ruth locked her gaze on the youngest of her three brothers. Though Micah had only beaten him into the world by five minutes, the older twin never let it go.

Malachi's hands flashed as he signed a response.

Ruth laughed. "That's more like it. And yes, as the eldest of the four of us, I am closest to being an old lady. But I still hope I never get this obsessed with crocheted...whatever these are all over the tables. That said, a cat isn't necessarily a bad idea. It'd at least be company."

"It's not our fault you pulled up stakes and moved west." Jonah frowned. "I still say you should've just sold the thing. What was Naomi thinking, leaving you a bed and breakfast in her will? A bed and breakfast in *Idaho*. Why was she even in Idaho?"

Ruth knew the answers to all of those questions, though they made little sense most days. Her best friend since kindergarten had tended toward eccentric even then. Losing her parents had pushed her right over the edge. "I'm pretty sure Idaho was the only possible place where Jaden wouldn't follow. I'm also fairly certain Naomi didn't plan to die."

Micah frowned. "Sorry. But why couldn't you wait for one of us to be free to come along?"

"Because she's booked through the spring. And the people coming to experience the wonders of nature available within an easy drive of Arcadia Valley shouldn't have to change their plans simply because cancer..." Ruth's throat closed around the rest of her sentence and her eyes filled. She breathed in and blinked. No more crying. She gulped. "Anyway. We've been through this. I'm staying. At least through the spring and summer. Then, I guess we'll see."

Malachi tugged on Micah's sleeve and he signed rapidly. Ruth squinted at the screen, but her youngest brother wasn't fully in range. Micah grinned, nodding. "Mal has a great idea. He's got some vacation that he's owed. As do I. We'll come out and help. What do you think?"

"Really? You're sure?" Her heart leapt in her chest. Having her brothers here, even if it was just two of the three, would be amazing.

"We're sure." Micah punched Jonah's arm. "What about you? Got any time saved up?"

Jonah nodded. "Yeah. I'll talk to my boss tomorrow. Be careful, Ruth. I don't like this."

"Worry wart. It's gonna be fine. Naomi loved it here."

"You two were always so similar...I guess you probably will, too." Jonah's shoulders slumped. "Don't be a stranger."

"You either. Come soon, okay?" Ruth stared at her brothers standing shoulder-to-shoulder in the tiny screen. They were her walls of support. When they weren't making her crazy. She blew them a kiss and hit end.

AFTER STOWING her luggage in the small owner's suite and running into town for a few groceries, it was time to get down to business. Armed with the instructions from Naomi's attorney, Ruth perched in front of the computer that had been stashed in the back corner of the kitchen. Why it wasn't in the rooms set aside for the owner of the B&B was something she didn't understand, but she could worry about that later. For now, she needed to get into the reservation system and the email to make sure she had the dates right for her first set of guests.

Something banged against the back door. Ruth jolted.

Heart pounding, she leaned back and eyed the window. The mostly sheer and entirely too-frilly curtain barely hid the shape of what was absolutely a man. Fixing a polite smile on her face, she crossed to the door and pushed aside the curtain. Her eyebrows lifted and she raised her voice, praying it would carry through the glass.

"Can I help you?"

The man frowned. "Who are you?"

"I own the B&B. Who are you?"

He shook his head. "Where's Naomi? Go tell her Corban's here, would you?"

How did he not know? Ruth flipped the dead bolt and tugged the door open a crack, leaning her weight against it so she could slam it shut if she needed. Not that it would be much defense when the top half of the door was glass. But it might give her a few seconds to grab her phone and run. "How do you know Naomi?"

"I'm her neighbor. I live over there." Corban gestured vaguely toward the farm across the road. But she hadn't seen a farmhouse and had assumed it was just a set of fields that belonged to someone who lived elsewhere. However farms worked. "Not that you need to know, but I've been in Florida settling my parents' estate. Naomi knows all this. Could you either let me in or go get her? I brought her the citrus she asked me for, and some avocados that she didn't ask for, but I remembered she loves them and these are huge."

Ruth sighed and opened the door. "You'd better come in. Why don't you go through to the parlor, Corban, was it? I made some lemonade."

He bent, his muscles flexing under his shirt as he lifted a

crate off the step with what appeared to be no effort whatsoever. "Where should I put the fruit?"

"Um. On the counter, I guess. Lemonade?"

He shrugged one shoulder. "Why not? You never said who you were."

Ruth took two tall glasses down from the cabinet by the sink. She filled them with ice at the refrigerator, poured the lemonade, and then decorated the rims with a transparent slice of lemon. "Let's go sit."

Another frown etched lines in his forehead, but he strode out of the kitchen. Ruth followed. Even frowns couldn't mar his good looks. He was older than her by several years, if she had to guess. But not more than forty. At thirty-three, that wasn't too much. Oh, good grief, what was she thinking? He'd probably had an eye on Naomi and now Ruth was going to have to break his heart.

He accepted the lemonade, his eyebrows lifting as he took a sip. "That's good. Thank you."

She couldn't miss the implication that he hadn't expected it to be good. Rude man. Ruth cleared her throat as she sat. Maybe it was better to blurt it out and be done. "Naomi passed away three weeks ago."

Corban stared at her, his mouth open in a tiny *O*. Slowly, his lips came together and the furrows in his forehead deepened. He set the glass down with a *thunk* on the antique table by his elbow, completely missing the lace doohickey that would protect the wood. "I'm sorry. What?"

Ruth's fingers itched to move the glass but she willed herself to stay still, perched on the edge of the settee. "She had cancer. And apparently never told anyone. I've been her best friend since kindergarten, we talk every week, and she only told me she was sick when it was clear that treatment wasn't a viable option. Her obituary was in the local paper."

"I told the guys watching the farm to read and recycle them. Nothing ever happens around here that's worth saving a newspaper. I'm not even sure why I still subscribe, except that Ernie's been a family friend for so long. She'd been acting odd. I knew I should have pushed."

"You two were close?" Ruth watched his face. He looked shocked, certainly, but not as destroyed as a man in love should be.

"Not like you mean." He offered a slight smile. "Though there were plenty of old ladies at church who were hopeful. No, Naomi was like a little sister to me. When she bought this place so my parents could move south, it seemed natural to keep an eye on her at first. And then..." He shrugged. "Then we were friends."

"Naomi could make anyone into a friend." Ruth's heart cracked open a little wider. How was she supposed to go through life without her? "I'm sorry you had to find out from me."

Corban nodded and stood. "I'll be on my way. I...my number's in her book. If you ever need anything, just give a shout."

"Thanks." He probably hadn't heard her, given that he'd been striding into the hall before she'd managed to get the word out. The kitchen door slammed.

Ruth sagged against the back of the stuffy little couch and took several long swallows of her lemonade. She was going to make a success of her friend's business. She had to. For Naomi, and for herself. And handsome, abrupt neighbors weren't going to get in her way.

2

C orban tucked his hands in his pockets as he trod
through the fields back toward the farmhouse. The
winter wheat looked like it was doing well. Should be
a good harvest, come mid-July. Depending. The other fields
were waiting. He could almost feel them waking up, getting
ready for another year. He was going to have to decide what to
do sooner than later. Prices weren't what they used to be.
Neither were costs. Though the two had traveled in opposite
directions, and not beneficial ones. He could get into cattle,
maybe sheep, but...he shook his head and paused to squat down
and take a handful of brown soil, letting it run through his
fingers. Animals. He wasn't a rancher.

Dusting his hand on the back of his jeans, he glanced back at
the bed and breakfast. Naomi should've told him. Though, timing-
wise, maybe she'd realized the end was coming around the same
time his parents had been in the accident and hadn't wanted to
add to his burden. That'd be just like her. She'd held everything
close to the vest. But she had mentioned Ruth a time or two. One
corner of his mouth curved as he continued toward the house.
The woman hadn't ever given him her name, but she had to be

Ruth. Naomi's description had been unmistakable. And she'd been right, Ruth was just his type. In looks, at least. Light brown hair that matched her eyes and that tiny sprinkle of freckles across her nose. She had girl-next-door written all over her. That suited him just fine. She could work on being a bit more welcoming to strangers though, particularly if she was going to be an innkeeper.

The chickens cackled at him as he walked past the coop. He paused to make sure they had everything they needed before he headed inside. He opened the fridge and grabbed the pitcher of iced tea one of the ladies from church had sent over yesterday, along with a box that held six casseroles. How was he supposed to eat his way through six casseroles in any useful amount of time? They'd gone in the freezer to worry about another day. The tea though, that hit the spot, so he kept it out. His mom used to brew a big jar of tea on the porch in the summer. It was just the thing after a long day in the fields. He should check and see if the container of mint she'd cultivated was still around, get back into the habit of tea. Maybe take some over to his new neighbor.

He smiled. Now that was an idea. He could always see how she was settling in, be neighborly. People were neighborly still, weren't they?

Corban sighed and filled his glass before sitting at the kitchen table. What was the point? He was thirty-six and had it on reasonably good authority—if you considered the bulk of the dateable women in Arcadia Valley to be reasonable or an authority—that he simply wasn't husband material. He was boring. He could hear his mother's voice in his head, chastising him for worrying about what short-sighted women said to him. At least he could thank God he'd had a good relationship with his parents while they were around. He swallowed the lump in his throat.

Was he boring? Maybe. He was...content. The farm was paid for. He made enough money most years to set a chunk of his income aside for the future. And he liked the quiet, the routine of farming. He'd ventured off to college, but even then the farm had called to him. There'd never been any pull to go do anything else, try anything else. He'd learned about organic farming in school and had, gradually, worked on his dad to transition their practices. In the end, it had been worthwhile. Even Dad had agreed.

And now it was all up to him. The last DeWitt to work the family farm.

He frowned, drained his tea, and stood. Enough moping. Thinking about the loss of his parents was making him maudlin. There was work to be done, and he'd best get to it.

CORBAN SWIPED sweat out of his eyes and cut the engine on his tractor. He'd worked his way to the back of the fields, getting ready for planting. He'd had to pause here and there to work out rocks, but if he was able to keep up the pace, the ground would be ready right on time. His gaze drifted across the road. How was Ruth settling in? The B&B looked as it always had. The gardens were just starting to send up some shoots, but the overall landscaping was evergreen hedges. His mother had wanted low maintenance and color year-round. She'd gotten it. They could use a trim though. *Hmm.*

He hopped down from the tractor and crossed the road before he could talk himself out of it. His jeans were dusty, but that was to be expected. Still, he'd go around the back to avoid mucking up the company rooms.

He smiled. Ruth had been so surprised when he'd knocked

yesterday. Maybe she'd be in a more hospitable mood today. He wouldn't say no to another glass of her lemonade.

Corban tapped on the glass in the kitchen door and tucked his hands in his pockets.

"Come in."

His eyebrows lifted. She just invited someone in, without knowing who it was? They were rural, and friendly, here in Arcadia Valley, but still. He pushed open the door and stepped in, pausing on the rag rug that now decorated the floor. "You shouldn't just call out like that."

Ruth glanced up as she continued kneading the mass of dough on the counter in front of her. She nodded toward the monitor of the computer in the corner of the room that displayed a clear view of the approach and kitchen door. "I saw it was you. I have another eight minutes of kneading before I can set this aside to rise. What can I do for you—Corban, right?"

He nodded. She had delicate hands. How were they strong enough to work dough like that? "I noticed the hedges out front need trimming. I used to do that for Naomi, and for my mother, before that. I thought I'd offer to continue."

"That's very thoughtful. Thank you." Ruth frowned. "I'm not sure where the gardening tools are."

"There's a shed out back. I can show you, later, if you like. It has all your snow removal equipment, too." Corban cleared his throat. "So that's a yes, then?"

"Can I pay you?"

"Oh, no. I just enjoy doing it. So...yes, then?"

"Yes."

He bobbed his head and left the kitchen, rounding the back of the house to the shed. The trimmers were right where they should be, as was the extension cord. He carried them out front and got to work. Across the road, the tractor looked lonely. But his work wasn't suffering, and this was a way to get to know the enigma who now ran his mother's old B&B. She was pretty, but he couldn't quite decide if she had a personality in there at all. Maybe she was just shy.

As he shaped the final curve on the last rounded bush, Ruth stepped out of the front door. The sun hit her hair. *Whoa.* Where he'd first seen plain brown, there was now a riot of color as red and blonde competed to shine. His breath caught in his chest. Corban flicked the trimmer off and lowered it.

"I thought you might be thirsty. I brought some orange juice."

He smiled, set down the tool, and crossed to the stoop. "Thanks."

"I came into a large box of citrus yesterday."

Corban laughed. "Sorry about that. I should've asked if you wanted it."

Ruth shrugged and looked out across the yard. "Thankfully, Naomi had a juicer. Most of it is in the freezer now. This looks much better. Thank you."

"You froze it? Doesn't that defeat the purpose of having fresh?" Corban took a long drink, the cool juice soothed his throat.

"Well, it wouldn't still be fresh by the time my first guests arrive in two weeks. So it was that or let it rot. This way I can use it in smoothies, sauces, or thaw it back out to serve as juice. And the peels are soaking in vinegar, which will make a nice cleaning product after it steeps for a while."

Who knew? Corban drained the glass and handed it back. "Sounds like you've got it covered, then. And the bread?"

She smiled. "Should be out of the oven in another twenty minutes. Would you like to hang around a bit and have a slice?"

It was tempting. Corban glanced over where his tractor waited and the pull of duty won. "I wish I could. I need to get back to the fields."

"Oh. Of course you do. I'm sorry."

"Don't be. This was a nice break. I'll just put the trimmer away and—"

"Leave it. I can get it. I—thank you. Really."

Corban shook his head and unplugged the trimmer. "It's not a problem. Appreciate the juice."

"Are you sure I can't pay you?" Ruth hurried behind him.

"I'm sure. I've been doing this since Mom first opened the place. Your friend let me keep on doing it. I'm happy to continue with you." He deposited the equipment in the shed and closed the door, tugging on the handle to be sure the latch caught. It had a tendency to pop open in the wind if it didn't catch just right. When he turned around, he nearly plowed into her. He grabbed her arm to steady her as she jolted. When their eyes met, he drew in a breath. "Beautiful."

Red stole across her cheeks and she looked away as she stepped back, clearing her throat. "Sorry. I'll just, um, thanks again. Bye."

He stood still as she turned and fled around the corner of the house. A door slammed. She must've gone in the kitchen. Corban rubbed the back of his neck. He hadn't meant to say it out loud, but that didn't change the truth of the statement.

CORBAN LEANED back in the rocker and propped his feet on the rail of his front porch. His Australian Shepherd, Spock, flopped on the deck nearby. The sun was just starting to sink on the horizon. Maybe it was a little cool for porch-sitting, but the walls had been closing in on him inside. He ought to find something for dinner, but it could wait.

The crew was all lined up to come back, so that was one less thing to worry about. He hadn't been sure they would. His dad had hired the bulk of them, and even though Corban had been in charge for going on ten years now, five of those with his parents in another state, the guys all called it his dad's farm. Now, with Dad gone, would they finally realize he was the one in charge? Did it matter? Not really. They still took instruction from him. It just always seemed like they were waiting for him to go and double-check.

A small sedan pulled into his driveway. Spock lifted his head off his feet. Corban sighed. He didn't recognize the vehicle, but he also didn't need another casserole or someone else coming to pay their respects. The ache in his heart had settled to a manageable level, as long as people didn't go around poking at it. If only his mother hadn't raised him to be hospitable, he could send them on their way.

The door opened and Ruth slipped out.

Corban pursed his lips. Maybe it wasn't going to be so bad after all. "Evening."

She straightened and nearly dropped whatever it was she had in her hands. "Oh. Hi. I'm sorry to just drop by. I brought you some bread."

He cocked his head to the side. "Thanks. Why don't you come on in and we can have a slice in the kitchen."

"I don't want to..."

Corban stood and grabbed the screen door, holding it open. Spock scurried through, disappearing into the house.

Ruth frowned, but she shut the car door and crossed to the porch. "You're sure I'm not interrupting?"

"I'm sure." Corban breathed in the subtle fragrance of yeast and oranges that seemed to float around her. "Kitchen's straight back."

She nodded and entered.

He let the screen slap closed behind him and followed as she picked her way across the gleaming wood floor. He hated polishing the wide planks, but they'd been his mother's pride and joy.

"This is just what a farmhouse should be." Ruth set the bread down on the kitchen table and looked around. "You must love it here."

"I do. Would you like me to put the kettle on? I have some tea...I think." His mother had kept one cupboard full of various teas—bags, loose, she loved it all. She'd taken some south when they'd moved, but had left the bulk here so she'd remember to come visit. Like she'd ever forget. He probably still had a good selection. Somewhere.

The smile lit her face, changing it from simply pleasant to almost beautiful. "That's okay. Water would be fine."

"I know I have some lemonade. It's not as good as yours. I get those tubs of powder at the grocery store. Not sure there were any real lemons harmed at any point in the process of making it. But it tastes fine."

Ruth chuckled. "That sounds good, too. Can I help?"

"Oh. No. Just have a seat." Corban ran a hand through his hair. Was he really this rusty when it came to entertaining? He crossed to the cupboards and pulled down two tall glasses. He snagged the pitcher from the fridge and filled them with the electric yellow liquid before setting them on the table. He slid a knife out of the block on the counter, collected two plates and a cutting board, and sat across from her. "Is this the loaf you were working on when I stopped by?"

Ruth sipped from the glass and winced. "Wow. That's sweet. No, that was just a simple sourdough. After you did the hedges, I wanted to do something special, so I played around with one of my grandmother's *challah* recipes."

He unwrapped the loaf and pulled his hand back. "That looks too nice to cut up."

"Please." Ruth shook her head and reached for the knife. "It's a simple braid."

Simple? The bread was a shiny golden brown, and the pattern looked far more intricate than a braid. He poked the middle of the slice when she slid it toward him. "Raisins?"

"And some nuts. You can eat nuts, right? I always forget about nut allergies." Ruth sawed through the bread and put a slice on the second plate.

"No allergies here. *Challah* you said? I'm not sure I've ever had it before. I usually get my bread at the grocery store." Corban took a bite. It was tender, eggy, and not overly sweet, despite the fruit and nuts. "This is good."

"You sound surprised."

"No. I just didn't know what to expect." With the bread or the baker.

uth smiled. Now what? Was she supposed to leave? She glanced down at the slice on her plate. Probably not time to leave just yet. He'd asked her in and offered to share. She pulled off a piece and popped it in her mouth. It had risen well, at least, but it needed...something. Maybe there was a reason challah wasn't usually mixed with anything sweet. She'd had success transforming other traditionally savory breads.

"Are you okay?" Corban's fingers rested light on her hand.

"Sorry. I was thinking about the bread. It's not as good as I was hoping it'd be. You don't have to keep it. It won't hurt my feelings."

He pulled the loaf closer and cut off another slice. "Nope. This is mine. Maybe I'm not a connoisseur, but I think this is quite tasty. You play around with recipes a lot?"

Her cheeks warmed. "Not as much as I'd like these days. I'm hoping the B&B gives me a chance to get back to it. I found a big tin of wheat berries and a mill when I was poking through the cupboards and figured maybe it was a sign."

"Naomi got that from me maybe three months back. Never

did say what she wanted it for. Must've been right before she found out she was sick."

Or she'd already known and had been planning for when Ruth would take over. Her friend had been just sneaky enough to do something like that. They'd had several conversations where Ruth had lamented the lack of time for baking in her life. As much as she appreciated having it now, she'd give it all up to have her best friend back. "Guess so. I'm sorry about your parents."

"Thanks." Corban shifted in his chair. "So tell me this, why take on the B&B? Why not sell it?"

Ruth sighed. "Now you sound like my brothers. I don't have anything holding me to the D.C. area. Well, nothing other than them. And they understand. Mostly. This feels like a second chance. Plus, I don't want to let Naomi down."

"I know a little about that. Have you run a hotel before?"

Why was this starting to feel like an interview? Sure, his mother had sold it to Naomi, but she'd owned it free and clear, hadn't she? Ruth picked at the crust of the bread in front of her. "I have, in fact. Five years ago, I opened a small inn on the outskirts of D.C. I sold it three years ago."

"Oh, wow. And since then?"

He had to ask. "A little of this and that. What about you? Have you always wanted to farm?"

He smiled and her heart skipped a beat. It was probably good he didn't unleash that too often. "No. But by the time I was halfway through college, I realized it was where I was meant to be, which was good since I'd been planning to come back anyway. It just meant that I came back excited and ready to make it my own instead of dragging my feet and fighting my dad the whole time. I'm grateful God settled my heart. There's nothing worse than pulling in the opposite direction of where He's leading."

What would it be like to know your place and be comfortable in it? She'd get there someday. She had to. The B&B was a good start. Even with the Victorian decor, it already felt more like home than her apartment in D.C. had. Maybe this was God settling her heart. She could hope. "Can I be impertinent?"

He lifted his eyebrows. "Why not?"

"How old are you?"

He laughed. "That's not impertinent. It might be if I asked you, since I'm pretty sure you don't ask a lady that, but I don't mind. I'm thirty-six."

She grinned. "I'll make my grandmother, rest her soul, roll over in her grave and go ahead and answer what you were too polite to ask. I'm thirty-three."

"I figured that. Naomi said you were friends in kindergarten, and I know how old she is. Was." Corban sighed. "It's going to take some getting used to."

Ruth nodded and pushed back her chair. "I should probably go. Enjoy the bread."

Corban stood. "I will. Thank you. Come by anytime."

She smiled and held his gaze for the space of a few heartbeats before nodding. "Okay. You too. The door's always open. Well, probably not unlocked, but I'll let you in if you knock."

RUTH CRINGED at her reflection in the bathroom mirror. "I'll let you in if you knock?"

He had to think she was a psychopath. She dried her face with the hand towel and reached for her cell phone. She needed to talk to her brothers. She hadn't been away from them for this long in...ever.

Settled in the chair-and-a-half in what passed for the living room of her private quarters, Ruth punched in Micah's number. It only rang twice before he picked up.

"Heya sis. How's it going?"

Ruth smiled, her entire body relaxing. "Better now that I'm talking to you. I didn't think you'd be home on a Friday night. How about you?"

"Same old. I scheduled my time off though, so did Mal. We're still working on Jonah, but he'll figure something out. You know how he is."

Jonah was the most serious of the four of them. He had to weigh everything from as many angles as he could think up before he'd move. "Yeah. I miss you guys."

"As you should. You sure you don't want to sell and come back home?"

"To what? At least here I don't have the stink of failure clinging to me. I have a chance to make this work and prove that the debacle in Georgetown wasn't my fault."

"Prove to whom? No one who knows you—or the situation— thinks it was."

She clamped the phone against her ear with her shoulder and scrubbed her hands over her face. Maybe he was right. Maybe he wasn't. She couldn't say why it mattered so much, just that it did. "Maybe I do. I don't know. I'm terrified I'm going to mess this up. And I'm homesick. And the farmer across the way is entirely too handsome for his own good. And—"

"Whoa, whoa, whoa! Hold up. Handsome farmer? Maybe I need to move my tickets up."

Ruth squeezed her eyes shut. One of these days she was going to keep her brain one step—maybe two—ahead of her mouth when talking to her brothers. "No. It's not...it's nothing. Can we talk about something else?"

"Nope. I want to hear about the farmer who's making a play for my older sister."

"He isn't making a play. He's just friendly. And his mom used to run the B&B, so he has a vested interest."

"Uh huh. So you're making a play for him?"

"No." Oh gosh. Did Corban think that? The bread...she was just trying to be friendly. Why hadn't she just stayed home tonight?

"That was fast."

"Micah, come on. You know me."

"I know you're gun-shy. I know that if I meet Lars on the road, I'm likely to punch him in the nose. And I know that you deserve to find someone who loves you."

"You're sweet, Micah, but I'm—"

"Going to see what happens. You've already said he's handsome. Is he nice?"

He'd brought her oranges. Well, technically they weren't for her, but the fact that he'd think to bring oranges for anyone after being away to settle his parents' estate said a lot about him. And he'd trimmed her hedges, and cleaned up even after she'd told him not to bother. "Yeah, he is."

"A believer?"

"That I don't know. I want to say he has to be, given how he acts, the things he says, but I know better." Her only serious boyfriend, the man she'd planned to marry and wasted eight years of her life on, had proved that beyond a reasonable doubt. "I guess I'll ask him."

"That's the spirit. Hang in there. You don't have any guests for two weeks, right?"

"Actually, I got a last-minute reservation this afternoon. Even though the woman wants to stay for two weeks, I have plenty of room. She'll check in on Monday. It'll be good to be doing instead of sitting around waiting." Ruth rubbed her eyes.

"Well, save space for Mal and me, and hopefully Jonah, starting next Friday, too."

"That soon?" Would she have enough space with her brothers here? "You're going to have to share a room. Or hang with me in the owner's area. I think the couch pulls out."

"We'll make it work one way or another. Don't sweat it. Just think how fun it'll be to have us there. And you should text Ma. He's missing you. A lot."

She chuckled. "I will. Thanks. You're just what I needed tonight."

RUTH SMOOTHED the sides of her khaki A-line skirt. It was a little chilly, but it wasn't clear on the website if Grace Fellowship was a dress-up congregation, or if she could get away with slacks. Better to be overdressed than under. She pressed her lips together and took a deep breath. She could do this. It was no different than finding a new church in D.C. Easier, maybe. After all, the smaller community had to mean that people would want to get to know her. Didn't it? Not that she had to stick with the first church she visited. Arcadia Valley might be a small town, but there were still several options for worship.

The foyer was reasonably full of people milling around before the service started. There was a good mix of ages, and dress appeared to be whatever people wanted it to be. She didn't stick out one way or the other, and that did wonders for the butterflies in her belly. She smiled and nodded to people who made eye contact as she headed toward the worship center doors. Taking a bulletin from the usher, she stepped to the side and scanned the room. Her gaze landed on a familiar profile. What were the odds? Still, it would be nicer than sitting alone.

Ruth crossed the room and tapped Corban's shoulder. "Good morning. Are you—is this seat taken?"

He'd jolted when she touched him. Now he grinned and

stood, then stepped out into the aisle. "Not until just now. Please, have a seat. It's good to see you. How was your Saturday?"

She sat, arranging her Bible and purse on the seat next to her. "Good. I spent most of it cleaning, and did another experiment with the *challah*. I think it turned out better. I'm thinking I'll try it as French toast tomorrow morning. If it's good, I'll repeat it for a guest I have checking in tomorrow afternoon. What about you?"

"I ate entirely too much of the loaf you brought by on Friday while I planned out vegetable crops. Wheat is still my primary focus, but I've been doing well at the farmers' market the past couple of years and thought I might expand that a little this year, see how it goes." He turned, his knees bumping hers. "Are you free for lunch after the service?"

Heat radiated from the contact point of their legs and her thoughts scattered. She looked up and met his searching light blue eyes. Her mouth went dry. "I'm sorry...what?"

He smiled and her insides turned to jelly. "Lunch? After the service?"

Ruth nodded.

"Excellent." He looked like he was about to say more, but the music started up.

She swallowed. Did she just agree to a date? No. It was just a friendly lunch. He was looking out for the new girl in town. Right?

4

Corban hadn't had this many grasshoppers jumping around in his stomach since he worked up the courage to ask Janelle Jenkins to the senior prom. Of course, since she'd said no, he was already one step ahead with Ruth. The Sunrise Cafe was his usual after church spot. Should he have chosen something fancier? He blew out a breath. Too late. That was her pulling into a parking spot. He waved as she climbed from her car.

"Find it okay?"

She smiled and his heart did a lazy flip. "Easy, just like you said. Thanks for inviting me."

Corban pulled open the door and held it for her. "My pleasure."

They waited by the sign asking them to do just that until a woman approached with a smile. "Hi there, Corban. You want a table or a booth?"

He looked at Ruth. "Do you have a preference?"

For the briefest moment, she looked stricken, then she shook her head.

"Booth?"

"Right this way." The woman turned and headed across the bustling restaurant.

He waited for Ruth to sit before sliding in across from her and picking up his menu. "I like that church gets out early enough that I can get over here before they get too crowded. Since they just do breakfast and lunch, you can end up cutting it close if you're not careful."

She chuckled. "I'll keep that in mind. This is the kind of place my brothers would love. I'll have to bring them when they come visit."

"How many do you have?"

"Three. Jonah, Micah, and Malachi. Mom used to tease Mal that he'd almost ended up named Nahum but Dad talked her out of it at the last minute."

"Lucky miss."

"Completely. Though I've always half-wished Mom had been reading Esther when I was born, instead of Ruth." She shrugged and closed her menu.

"You decided already?"

"They have a Reuben. Anytime I see that, I have to try it. It's a compulsion." Pink tinged her cheeks and she glanced down at the table.

"It's a good choice." Corban pursed his lips and nodded. "In fact, I think I've changed my mind. Three brothers. What's that like?"

"Noisy. They're all younger than I am. Jonah just turned thirty. Micah and Malachi are twenty-eight. And they still pound on each other regularly. They insist it's a sign of affection. I just try to stay out of the way."

He couldn't quite picture it. "That sounds kind of fun. I'm an only child. We always had dogs, though. I used to love to lie on the floor and wrestle with them. Broke more than one of my mom's vases that way."

The server appeared at their table with water, took their orders and left.

Ruth fidgeted with her glass. "Did your parents have any siblings?"

"One each. They're spread out around the country now though. Cousins too. We get together every five years or thereabout. I don't always make it out. They forget I'm pretty tied to the farm in the summer and fall, but I do my best."

Ruth reached out and briefly rested her fingers on the top of his hand. Electricity sizzled up his arm. Did she feel it? She had to. "I'm sorry."

"Thanks. But it's really okay. I've been alone on the farm for five years now. And it's not like I'm ever really alone. I have Spock, obviously, and the crew's in and out practically all year, between planting, covering up crops if we're looking at a late freeze, and the staggered harvest. Dad always said he should put a revolving door in the farmhouse."

She smiled and moved her hand. The place where her fingers had rested was cold without her touch. "And I'm just across the way, if you ever get lonely in the evenings. If the Fairview is anything like the place I had in D.C., guests will keep to themselves pretty well. So while I have to be around, in case they have questions, I'm still going to be up for a visit from a friend."

A FRIEND. Corban grinned. It was a place to start and he was good with it. He rubbed Spock's head. The dog moaned and leaned into his touch. "I know it, buddy."

"Still talking to your dog, I see."

"Emerson?" Corban launched to his feet and took the steps from the porch in one long stride. "Emerson Hadley? What are you doing here? You swore you'd never set foot in Arcadia Valley again."

The tall, lanky man shook his head. "God has a unique sense of humor."

"What do you mean? You're not just visiting?"

"Nope. Seems the wife found out they needed a surgeon at the hospital in Twin Falls. But she didn't want to live there, guess she got nostalgic for home. We put an offer on the old Madison place and the real estate agent says it's a pretty sure thing." Emerson hooked his thumbs in the belt loops of his jeans. "Still running the farm, I see."

Corban slung his arm around his friend's shoulders. "Sure am. Come on in, I made some sun tea."

"Turning domestic, too? You need a woman, Corb."

Corban winced. The nickname was the only thing about their relationship that he hated. "Working on it, *Em*. How old are the boys now?"

"Seven and five."

Corban shook his head and held the screen open. "And you still like being a stay-at-home-dad? Never pictured that as your role."

Emerson grinned. "I love it. Those boys...they're smart as whips. Homeschooling is a bigger adventure than twelve hours in an attorney's office ever was. I still keep my bar membership up, here and in Washington, but I don't know that I'll ever go back to full-time practice."

His best friend was an at-home dad and homeschooler. Not at all what they'd talked about long into the night when they were in high school. Whereas Corban was pretty much right where he'd predicted he'd be. Only difference was now he was here by choice. "That's great. It looks good on you. Have a seat. I'll get the tea. Need a snack?"

"Have I ever turned down food?"

"Thought maybe now that you were pushing forty you'd be slowing down some."

"Kids keep me young and in shape. What'cha got? Is that homemade? You're baking bread now? You seriously need a woman."

"Ha ha." Corban set what was left of the *challah* on the table with a tub of butter and got two glasses and the pitcher of tea. "This is from the new owner of the Fairview."

"Your mom's B&B? I thought that lady, oh, what was her name? You mom was convinced the two of you should end up together."

"Naomi. And it was just mom. Neither Naomi nor I agreed. She passed away unexpectedly and left it to Ruth in her will. I'm finding it hard to mind that she chose someone like Ruth to take over."

"Oh?" Emerson studied Corban for a minute before taking a slice of bread. "Mmm. Knows her way around the kitchen. You like her."

It wasn't a question. Emerson knew him well enough to know that if Corban brought a girl up, he was interested. But it was too early to say. "We've got a good start at being friends. That's enough for now."

Emerson nodded. "Don't move too slow. I'd like my boys to have some playmates."

Corban scoffed. "It's unlikely. And even if it does happen, it's more like your boys can babysit. But we'll see what God has."

"You were always more content than me. I envied you that. Still do."

Corban snapped his mouth shut. What did a guy say to something like that? He reached for the last slice of bread and dipped his knife into the butter. "The Madison place, huh?"

"So it seems."

Corban grinned. "It's good to have you home, man."

5

"Welcome to the Fairview B...Jaden?" Ruth glanced down at the appointment book on her tablet. That wasn't the name on the reservation.

"Hi, Ruth. Hope you don't mind, but I had my friend do the booking. I wanted to surprise you."

Ruth fixed a smile in place. "You succeeded. What brings you to Arcadia Valley?"

"Oh, you know, just had to come and see where my sister spent her last days. I guess I'm looking for closure. We were never close, not as close as I wanted to be. I just hoped that staying here might help it all make sense somehow." Jaden's eyes filled with tears and she looked down. Then she ruined the effect by glancing up through her lashes to see Ruth's reaction.

"I hope you can find that. I know Naomi would want it for you. Let me get your bags and I'll show you to your room. I put you upstairs in the garden room. It's the largest and has a nice sitting area, plus a good view of the backyard." Ruth took the handle of Jaden's suitcase and hefted it before crossing to the stairs. What had the woman packed? She forced her breathing to steady as she reached the upstairs hall. "Here we are. There's a binder with information on the various activities around. If you have any questions, or you'd like me to make you some reservations, just let me know. Breakfast is at eight."

Jaden scrunched her nose as she looked around the room. "How quaint. What do you recommend for dinner?"

"There are a number of local restaurants. Most of them have a menu in the binder. Or you can go into Twin Falls if you'd like something fancier."

"Is there a pizza delivery?"

"Yes, of course. You'll find their number in there, too. They give guests a ten percent discount. Just be sure to mention it."

"Great. I'll let you know if I need something."

Ruth nodded and turned from the room, pulling the door closed behind her. Not only would Jaden do just that, Ruth imagined it would be a frequent occurrence. She trudged down the stairs and went into the kitchen where she pulled out her sourdough starter. Naomi had always regretted the relationship she had with her younger sister, but nothing she'd done had ever mended things. What could Jaden possibly want?

If the twisting in Ruth's gut was any indication, it wasn't going to be anything good.

RUTH POUNDED the risen dough down and tossed it onto the floured counter. Jaden still hadn't come down from her room, even though it was approaching dinner time. An optimist might assume that was a good sign, but Ruth knew Jaden too well. Even if she hadn't grown up watching her sabotage her sister, the stories Naomi had told would have been enough. Why was she here?

The glass in the kitchen door rattled at the knock. She flicked her gaze to the monitor and smiled, her heart lifting when she saw Corban. She brushed her hands off and strode to the door. "Hey. What brings you by?"

Ruth washed her hands and returned to the bread she was kneading, the silky, elastic dough soothing her nerves.

Corban came in and closed the door behind him. He cleared his throat. "I'm finished for the day and heading into town to meet an old friend who just moved back. I wondered if you'd like to join me. Us."

She looked down at the dough, her thoughts racing. She had a guest. Not just any guest, either. Jaden. She'd taken the precaution of locking the room to her private area, but there were still things in the public spaces that were small and could easily be slipped into a suitcase. Not that, from the weight of the thing at least, there was likely any room. "I'd better not. I have a guest and...it's complicated. I appreciate the offer."

He drew his eyebrows together. "What will you do for dinner?"

"I was going to throw some pasta together later. I found a nice block of parmesan at the store, so I thought I'd make an Alfredo." She paused and looked up. "Do you want to join me? Pasta is easy. Your friend could come."

"I don't...he's married, two kids."

Ruth shrugged. "I have a big dining room. Kids like pasta usually. But I'd probably make a salad, too. Maybe some garlic bread?"

Corban's stomach rumbled.

She laughed. "Is that a yes?"

"Let me give them a call." He tugged his cell phone out of his pocket and frowned at it for a minute before punching the numbers. "Hey, Emerson, it's Corban. Would you and Pam and the kids want to come to the B&B for dinner? Ruth can't get away and she was...yeah, sure...yep, the kids too...uh-huh...that's what she said. Okay, great. See you then."

"We're good?"

He nodded. "What can I do to help?"

"Let me just get this set aside to rise a second time and I'll figure it out." The pasta was no problem, she had plenty of that. But what was she thinking inviting a family of four that she'd never met to dinner? That was easy. She wanted to get to know Corban better, and any excuse would do.

"It seemed like a good idea at the time." Corban's cheeks were red, but he shrugged. "At least the tractor wasn't wrecked."

Emerson laughed. "Your dad about killed you, if I recall."

"That's true. Why are we telling these stories again?"

Ruth scooted away from the table. "I believe that might be my fault. But I can't quite say I'm sorry. It's been educational. We can move to the sitting room for dessert."

Pam winced and glanced at the two boys. "Are you sure? They're not...neat eaters."

"I'm sure. It's just dessert bread with honey-butter. I didn't have time for anything fancy." Ruth started stacking plates. "It'll be fine. Corban can show you where it is."

Without waiting to see what they'd do, Ruth carried the pile of plates into the kitchen and stopped in the doorway. Jaden was hunched over the computer, scowling. Thank the Lord Ruth had changed the password the day she arrived. She put every bit of ice she could muster into her voice. "Can I help you with something?"

Jaden gestured to the computer. "I need to check my email. You can let me log in so I can do that."

Ruth set the dishes in the sink. "I'm sorry, that's not one of the services we provide here. There's free Wi-Fi, the connection details are all in the guest folder in your room. But if you don't have a computer with you, perhaps you could try the library."

Jaden crossed her arms. "I don't feel like going out. Come on, Ruth, just let me use the machine. You're not using it."

"I'm sorry, but no. This area is off limits to guests, which is why there's a sign on the door marking it private."

"I'm hardly a guest, Ruth. We're practically sisters."

What was the woman after? "Jaden, you and I both know that's not true. Now, if you'll excuse me, I have company. You're welcome to join us for conversation in the lounge if you're not going out."

"You're going to regret this. This place should be mine. Naomi was *my* sister, not yours. No matter how you tried to steal her. You and your whole stupid family. But you're not going to get away with it this time." Jaden stormed out of the kitchen, plowing into Corban on her way through the door.

Ruth sagged against the counter and stared at the ceiling, blinking back tears.

"You okay?" Corban touched her shoulder. Part of her mind registered the shivers that worked their way down her arm, the rest focused on breathing in and out and not throwing something. "I mean, you're not. Obviously. I only caught a little at the end but...that lady's crazy. You know her?"

Ruth let out a little laugh. "She's Naomi's younger sister. They never got along. She hates me. I don't understand why she's here."

"Hey." Corban pulled her against his chest, slipping his arms around her.

Ruth breathed in his masculine scent and closed her eyes. Tears slipped down her cheeks and she fought against the flood pressing against her eyelids. She was not going to cry over this. This wasn't the first time Jaden had tried to disrupt Ruth's life. But it was going to be the last. She dragged in another deep breath and wrapped her arms around Corban, giving him a quick squeeze before stepping back. "Thanks."

"My pleasure."

She wiped her cheeks and forced a smile. "I like your friends. I can see why you're glad they're back in town."

"Emerson's good people. And Pam was made for him. They're peas in a pod."

Ruth opened the bread box on the counter and sighed. Half of the sweet loaf she'd baked this afternoon was missing. She pulled out the sourdough and the half-loaf. "Looks like Jaden helped herself to some bread while she was snooping."

"Don't worry about it. If that one's anything like what you gave me, it'll be great." He reached for the cutting board she'd arranged the bread on. "Let me get that."

"Corban." She touched his arm and held his gaze. "Thank you."

6

C orban stopped the tractor and looked across the road. He hadn't talked to Ruth since Monday night. He missed her. Which was dumb. But that woman who was staying with her was bad news. Ruth hadn't been willing to file a police report, saying Jaden hadn't actually threatened her. Maybe not, but he would've felt better. And yet he hadn't called or stopped by for three days. Was it because Emerson had ragged on him so much about having the hots for the innkeeper, as he so cleverly put it? Honestly, they weren't in high school anymore. Who said stuff like that at their age?

He whistled for Spock. The dog loped up. "Let's go visit our neighbor. You remember Ruth?"

Spock wagged his tail, his tongue lolling out the side of his mouth.

Corban stepped down from the tractor and patted his leg as they stepped into the road that separated the farm from the B&B. It had once all been owned by his family, but working both sides of the road had been too much for his dad when Corban was in college, so his mom had convinced Dad to diversify. Mom loved the Fairview. It had kept them in Arcadia Valley past the time Dad wanted to retire to Florida. Corban circled around the side to the kitchen door and knocked.

"It's open."

He pushed the door open and chuckled. She was up to her elbows in bread dough. "Spock's with me. Okay if he comes in?"

"Sure. I baked him some dog treats yesterday. I'd planned to bring them over tonight if you didn't stop by." Pink flooded her cheeks. "Not that I expected you. I was just hoping...I mean, it's always good to see you."

He hid a smile. She might regret her rambling, but it was good to hear he wasn't the only one attracted. Spock padded into the kitchen and sat by Ruth's feet. "I think he heard you talking about biscuits."

She laughed. "Give me a minute. I need to finish this and set it to proof, and then I'll get the tin down."

Corban leaned on the island and eyed the dough. "What is it today?"

"I mixed Asiago cheese in with my basic sourdough. We'll see how it goes, but I'm hopeful. I have a vision of a piece of toast with slightly gooey pockets of cheese spread throughout."

His mouth watered. "I'm available for testing whenever you need."

She grinned. "Do you have any feelings on sun-dried tomatoes?"

"Not particularly. Why?"

"Thought I might try them next." She slipped the ball of dough into a bowl, covered it with a towel, and stuck it in the corner of the kitchen. "This is the least drafty spot. If I keep baking like this, I might have to invest in a proofing drawer. And speaking of that, any chance I could buy some more wheat berries from you? I'm nearly through the bag Naomi had."

"Sure, I'll bring some over. Bake me another loaf of bread and we'll call it square. You're really grinding all your flour? Doesn't that take forever? Does it make that big of a difference?"

Ruth rinsed her hands and dried them, flipping the towel over her shoulder when she was finished. She opened a cabinet and stood on her tiptoes to grab a round red tin. "It doesn't take that long, I have a nice powered mill. And you tell me. Think about the last bread you got at the store."

He lifted his hands in defeat. There was no contest. "All right. You win. Are those cookies?"

Ruth shook her head and held out the bone-shaped biscuit to Spock. "They're dog treats, like I said. My baking really only extends to bread."

Corban plucked one from the tin and sniffed it. "There's nothing weird like liver in it though, right?"

"Nope. It's just probably blander than what you'd consider..."

He nibbled on one end.

"Okay then."

Corban tossed the biscuit toward Spock, who nipped it out of the air. "It's not bad. But you're right, bland."

The dog lay on the floor crunching happily on the treat, the second nestled between his paws.

"Your guest giving you any more trouble?"

Ruth shook her head. "She's been conspicuously absent the past two days. She comes down for breakfast, says nothing except please and thank you, and then disappears for the day. She's usually back around seven and heads straight up to her room. I've checked all the other rooms, they're still locked and don't look disturbed, and I haven't found her trying to snoop, but she's had the 'do not disturb' sign on her door every time I've gone up to freshen things, and even though I know she's out, I feel like I should respect that. I'm grateful my brothers and more guests arrive soon."

"Your brothers are coming out?"

Her smile lit up her face. "All three. I wasn't sure Jonah was going to be able to swing the time off, but he called and said to make sure I had room. I can't wait for them to get here. You're going to love them."

"I'm sure I will." Unless they were the over-protective types who'd try and scare him off. Would they object to a farmer courting their sister? Courting. Now that was a word you didn't hear every day. Was it what he was doing? That was something to think about. "When do they get here?"

"Saturday. New guests don't show up until Tuesday. Jaden's scheduled to leave next Friday. That can't come soon enough." She glanced toward the closed kitchen door. "I shouldn't say that. It's mean, but she makes me uneasy."

"Do you want me to bunk here? I could take one of the guest rooms so you aren't alone at night if you wanted. I'm happy to pay." He didn't want her thinking he was making a move. But he also didn't want her here alone if she was unsettled. "Or I could see if Emerson, Pam, and the boys wanted to move here from the hotel. They don't close on their house for another couple of weeks and Emerson's parents' house isn't really suited for the kids."

"Thank you. That's sweet. But I'm okay. My brothers will be here in two days. I can manage until then."

"If you change your mind, you know how to reach me."

She nodded. "You're in my cell. Have you started planting yet?"

"Next week, maybe, if the weather stays good. I can start putting in leeks, broccoli, cabbage, that sort of thing. I'll have to keep it covered, but it'll be good to get started."

"I'm already looking forward to having fresh produce in the summer."

He grinned. "Me too. Do you think, maybe, once your

brothers are settled, you'd be able to leave them in charge and come out to dinner with me?"

She blinked. "Dinner? Like a date?"

Heart pounding in his chest he nodded. "Like a date."

"Pam doesn't mind you hanging out with me tonight?" Corban opened a bag of chips and set it on the coffee table before dropping into one of the two recliners in front of the television.

Emerson shook his head. "She's got a later shift tonight, and her parents have been desperate to keep the boys overnight, despite their house being far from kid-friendly. Pam said why not give it a shot now, so we know how it'll work later if we want to try and plan something? I figure that's reasonable, seeing as I can run out on you without too much fuss if I need to."

Corban laughed. "Movie? Video game? What are you up for?"

"Video games? When did you get into that?"

"It's something to pass the time on nights when I don't feel like reading."

"That happens?"

"It's been known to, yes." Corban frowned at his friend. Just because a guy liked to read didn't mean he had no other interests. "Maybe you've been gone long enough that you've forgotten how rural we really are here."

"Just giving you a hard time. I'm up for a game. Especially if it's one I can't play with the boys. I get enough of those at home."

Corban pointed to the cabinet under the TV. "They're in there. Choose what you want and load it up. Want a soda?"

"Sure. Why not?" Emerson squatted by the TV and opened the door that hid the shelves underneath.

Corban ambled into the kitchen to grab drinks. He had a life. Maybe it wasn't a big city life, but he didn't live in the big city, did he? Emerson had spent the last ten years in Seattle, chasing the dreams he'd had since high school. And he'd still ended up right back in Arcadia Valley. Corban turned and stared out the kitchen window. It was dark enough that he couldn't see all the way to the Fairview. How was Ruth doing tonight? Had that woman—Jaden, wasn't it?—given her any trouble, or was she still keeping to herself? He'd nearly called her six times today, just to check in. And then he'd stopped because...why? When was the last time he'd been interested in a woman like this? Too long ago to count.

He grabbed two cans out of the fridge and carried them back to the living room. "So. What'd you choose?"

Emerson held up a case that featured warring post-apocalyptic treasure hunters. "Dude. I've been *dying* to play this. You've been holding out on me."

It was a solid game. He'd finished it right after it came out. What was that, two years ago now? Still, it had decent replay. "Load it up. I'll choose a different character than when I first played."

"We have to do this at least once a month now that I'm back in town. We had friends in Seattle, but it's not the same. As much as I wanted to get away, coming back? This is home. You know?"

Corban nodded. "I figured it out while I was still in college, but then, I've always been a little smarter than you."

Emerson snorted and brought the controller back to his seat. "Keep telling yourself that."

"You sure Pam isn't going to mind if you leave her alone on a Friday night once a month?"

"That's a fair point. We'll just have to find you a woman, then she and Pam can hang while we do. Or we can mix it up now and then and go out as couples. With both sets of grandparents in town, finding someone to watch the boys shouldn't be too big a deal." Emerson gave Corban a side-eyed glance. "Maybe that nice girl who's running the B&B now? What was her name?"

Heat flooded Corban's cheeks. "Ruth. As you already know. I see you haven't figured out subtlety yet, either."

Emerson snickered. "So? Spill."

"There's nothing to spill." Though she had agreed to go on a date with him. Was he supposed to tell his friend that? "Her brothers are coming tomorrow for a visit. We're going to go out when they're settled."

"Who's we? You, Ruth, and her brothers?"

Corban frowned and hit the start button. "No. Me and Ruth. Were you this dense in high school and I just didn't notice?"

"Probably. But I make life interesting and fun, so you keep me around. That's what Pam always says."

Corban laughed. "She isn't wrong. Hurry up and choose a character."

"Tell me this: when was the last time you were out on a date?"

"Who keeps track?"

"So...it's been awhile."

He shrugged. There was no need for his friend to know all the sad details of his non-existent dating life.

"If you need any tips, let me know." Emerson hit some buttons on his controller. "All right, I'm ready."

"When was the last time you went on a date again?"

"Hey, I take Pam out all the time."

"Not quite the same though, is it?" Corban activated the first quest. "I think I'll be okay."

"Don't screw it up, 'k? Pam and I both like her." Emerson

turned and arched his brow. "When was the last time Pam liked anyone you were interested in?"

Corban shook his head. Never. Even in high school, Pam had been a little mother. He could chalk up the end of two different relationships to Pam making it clear to the girls in question that they weren't good enough for him. "I'll keep that in mind."

7

"You're here!" Ruth threw her arms around Jonah and squeezed.

He returned the hug and grinned down at her. "Surprise. Though I'm guessing Micah spilled the beans."

"Was it a secret?" Micah bumped Jonah out of the way and pulled Ruth into his arms. "You're a sight for sore eyes."

Ruth laughed. "I haven't been gone that long. You can't possibly have missed me already."

Malachi's hands flashed as he spoke. "I did. You left me alone with these two morons."

"Hey. I resemble that remark." Micah punched his twin in the shoulder.

Ruth signed as she turned to Malachi. "Sorry about that. I think, once you look around, you'll understand why."

"Already do." Malachi slung one arm around Ruth's shoulders and looked around, not bothering to sign while he spoke. "Maybe the decorations aren't what you'd choose, but I can already see you fit here."

She let out a breath. That was it, exactly. Leave it to Mal to get it. To get her. For him to feel comfortable enough speaking without signing was huge, too. Since he'd lost his hearing after he learned to talk, he didn't have the tell-tale distinctiveness in his voice that many who were deaf did. But he'd always been self-conscious. When you coupled that with his quiet nature, you got a sensitive man who didn't say much. When he did speak, it was always worth listening. Ruth kissed his cheek. "I'm glad you're here. All of you. Come on, I'll take you up to your room and then show you around. Sorry you have to share, but it's..."

"Don't sweat it." Jonah reached for his duffel bag. "We'll be fine."

Micah shot Jonah a look. Jonah shook his head.

Ruth frowned. Whatever that was about they weren't saying yet. She'd pry it out of one of them sooner or later. "Before we go up I should warn you, Jaden's here. She keeps to herself, but you'll see her at breakfast. She's leaving on Friday. We'll have two new couples on Monday, so just be polite if she says anything, okay?"

Malachi rolled his eyes and grabbed his bag.

Micah pointed to the stairs. "We go up here, right?"

Fine. They weren't going to say anything. They wouldn't embarrass her. Not on purpose, at least. But Jaden...who knew what that girl was going to do? She'd been polite—mostly— since the first day. But Jaden hated Ruth's brothers even more than she hated Ruth. Having them here was wonderful, but the timing could've been better. Ruth gave herself a firm mental shake. That was enough. This was a business and she could be professional. So could her brothers.

"Here we are. It's the best I could do for the three of you. If it gets too cramped, someone can take the sofa in my rooms. It's not the most comfortable, but it's not awful." Ruth unlocked the door and pushed it open, revealing two twin beds with a roll-away bed folded against the wall. "You do have a private bathroom just through there. And if you keep the third bed folded during the day, it might not be too bad."

"It's great. I doubt we'll be in here much unless we're sleeping anyway. I was reading up on the area, there are some great rafting trips and hikes around here. Think you could get away and come along?" Jonah made puppy dog eyes.

Ruth chuckled. "That hasn't worked on me since you got taller than I am. Probably not, but you're welcome to go. There are brochures in the binder over by the phone. Some of the places give my guests a discount. We're a little before the real season, but I think a few operate as close to year-round as they can manage. Give 'em a call and see."

"You don't need us here?" Micah dropped his duffel on a bed.

"Whoa there, Sparky." Jonah reached over and grabbed Micah's duffel. "I don't think we've determined who gets a bed just yet."

Micah grinned. "Snooze you lose, man."

"Lose. Whatever, I'll just take..." Jonah frowned as he turned. "No. Way."

Malachi wriggled on the other bed and folded his arms behind his head. "Ahhh. Comfy."

Ruth fought to hide a smile. "You can always take my couch."

Jonah sighed. "We're alternating nights."

"Hello? Is anyone actually home?" Jaden's scorn-laden voice carried clearly down the hall.

Ruth winced. "I'll be right back. You three figure it out, okay?"

She stepped back into the hallway and fixed on a bright smile. "Did you need something, Jaden?"

Jaden scowled from the doorway of her room. "Someone needs to freshen in here."

"Of course. Were you planning to go somewhere today? I

usually do the rooms while the guests are out, if they don't have the 'Do Not Disturb' sign out."

"I'm leaving shortly. If I'd known the sign would keep you from freshening, I would've taken it in."

Ruth bit her tongue. What did she think the sign was for? Don't disturb unless you're going to change the sheets? "I'll update the material in the guest folder to make that more clear."

Jaden huffed, turned, and slammed the door in Ruth's face.

Ruth closed her eyes and started counting.

Micah let out a low whistle.

She spun, eyes wide, and gestured for him to go back in his room. Crossing the distance, she held up a finger before any of her brothers could speak. "She's a paying guest. It's not a big deal."

"Ruth. Please." Micah frowned. "You shouldn't let her treat you that way. What did she think the sign was for, if not to keep you out?"

"I know that. You know that. But please, okay? I just want her to have the best possible experience here and then leave. Preferably without putting a nasty review online." Ruth twisted her fingers together, one ear listening for sounds in the hall. "Let it go."

"I...yeah, okay." Micah glanced at Jonah. "Maybe we shouldn't leave Ruth alone."

"Don't be silly. Go rafting and hiking. It's gorgeous out there. And maybe one night this week I could get you to hold down the fort?" Butterflies danced in her stomach. They were going to give her the third degree, but a date with Corban was worth that. He was so...there weren't words.

Malachi cocked his head to the side, signing quickly. "Got a hot date?"

Micah smirked.

Jonah laughed. "Right. Ruth doesn't date, remember?"

If the heat was any indication, her face was bright red. She chewed on her lower lip. "Actually. I do."

"You do what?" Jonah blinked.

She took a deep breath. Better to just spit it out. "I have a date. Or, at least, an open-ended offer for one. And I'd like to take him up on it."

"With who? You've only been here two weeks. Who's asking you out that fast?" Jonah's gaze bored into her.

"Gee, thanks, Jonah. You know just how to make a girl feel special. No wonder women are throwing themselves at your feet." Ruth stared at him until he broke eye contact.

"Sorry. I'm just surprised."

"Clearly. However, as I'm a grown woman—older than all three of you, I might add—I think that's my business. Let me know when you're available to watch things, would you? I have a room to freshen and some bread to bake." Ruth resisted the urge to slam the door behind her as she left their room. They meant well, but that didn't stop it from being annoying. Even when she'd been a teenager, her brothers had been over protective. Mom and Dad had said it was because they loved her and because brothers were supposed to look out for their sisters. Maybe so. But it didn't stop it from being annoying.

"Hey. I was hoping I'd see you again this morning." Corban tucked his hands in his pockets and smiled at Ruth.

Her heart lifted and she smiled back. "Wouldn't miss it. I liked it last week, didn't see any reason to look elsewhere."

"Did your brothers come with?"

"They're around somewhere. Jonah said something about getting an extra bulletin and the twins tagged along." Which was weird, now that she said it out loud. What were they up to?

She cleared her throat. "I was thinking Tuesday? Does that work?"

A grin split his face, causing little dimples in his cheeks. Her heart fluttered. It was potent. "Yeah. Tuesday's great. Five?"

She nodded, her mouth suddenly dry.

"There you are." Jonah slipped his arm around Ruth's shoulders. Micah and Malachi arranged themselves behind her.

Ruth fought a wince. They'd formed the protective circle. "I told you I'd be right here. Guys, this is Corban DeWitt. He owns the farm across the road from the B&B, which his mother actually started. Corban, my brothers."

Jonah stuck out his hand. "Jonah. Pleasure to meet you."

Micah and Malachi followed suit.

"Can I take you all to lunch as a welcome to town? I know your sister's happy to have you here. She's been missing you."

Ruth chuckled. He'd just rolled right along with things. Most guys went running when her brothers started. "Now that they're here, I can't remember why that was."

"Family's good to have around." Corban nodded to the men ranged around her. "Especially when you're as tight knit as the four of you clearly are. I think it's great you came out."

"Me too. And I'd love to go to lunch with you." Ruth turned to her brothers. "You coming?"

"I like to eat." Micah jabbed Jonah with his elbow. "Lead on."

"Have you been to The Jukebox yet?"

Ruth shook her head. "I've heard it's good though. It's one of the few positive comments Jaden's made."

"Head down Main. You can't miss it. The front of the building is a giant neon jukebox."

Jonah winced.

Corban shrugged. "The food's better than that suggests."

Ruth headed for her car, not bothering to check if her brothers were following. She'd avoided the third degree yesterday, but it was coming. Jonah's expression made that clear. With Dad gone, Jonah took the idea of head of the house very seriously. Shouldn't that make him happy about the prospect of his sister marrying and having a family? Her hand stilled on the handle of her car door. Marrying? She and Corban hadn't even been out on a real date. And yet...she could picture it. He was exactly the kind of man she'd been praying for her whole life.

"So. Farmer next door?" Jonah shook his head. "Could you be any more of a cliché?"

"How is that a cliché?" Ruth checked traffic before zipping onto the road.

"You moved to Idaho and fell for a farmer. That's pretty much the definition of cliché." Micah shifted in the back seat. "That said, he seems nice enough. And he likes you a lot and doesn't bother to hide it, which is major points in my estimation."

Ruth's heart raced. Was that true? She didn't see it. Was she not looking? Or was she so busy trying to make sure he didn't see just how interested she was that she missed signals he sent? She wet her lips. "Glad I have someone's approval. Can you mind the fort on Tuesday so we can go out?"

Micah laughed. "You owe me twenty, Jonah. But yes, the three of us will be happy to mind the store."

"You bet on me?" Ruth glanced at Jonah. "What was the bet?"

Malachi touched her shoulder with the gesture he used when he knew she was going to be annoyed.

"Tell. Me. Now." She pulled into a parking spot in front of the restaurant and cut the engine before turning to glare at Jonah. "You bet I was making up the date, didn't you?"

Jonah shrugged. "It didn't seem all that likely that you'd actually have a date this soon."

"I oughta make you walk home." Ruth pushed open the car door.

"Hey." Jonah touched her arm. "I'm sorry."

She thawed a little. But not completely. "You're still buying my lunch."

Jonah chuckled. "If Corban lets me, you're on. But I'm betting on him. Micah's not wrong. And that's the only thing that kept me from squeezing his hand off at church. He likes you. A lot. So if you like him back, you might want to let that show."

RUTH SANK her hands into the bowl and squeezed the ingredients together. They gradually formed into a ball and she turned it out onto the floured counter before pushing with the heels of her hands, flopping it back onto itself, giving it a turn, and repeating the process. It was mindless now, her hands and arms already accustomed to the motions, which left her free to think.

Her brothers had been great at lunch. They seemed to genuinely like Corban. And he them. They'd all gone over to the farm. Apparently Corban had some video game they were desperate to try out. Who knew the man played video games? Was that just something everyone with a Y chromosome enjoyed? Ruth had come home, changed her clothes, and freshened Jaden's room since the woman was out and there was no sign on the door. But the sun dried tomatoes she'd found at the store were calling her name, as was the jar of Greek olives. Should she mix them together or make individual loaves? There was enough dough here for two, but not for three. She'd do them separately this time. Maybe tomorrow, if she had enough left over, she'd try combined.

The kitchen door opened and Jonah strode in. "Need a hand?"

"I thought you were playing video games with Corban?"

"The Ms are still over there. I thought I'd make sure you were okay. Besides, I figured you'd be making bread. I may be on vacation, but I'm still used to being on the line. I don't know what to do with myself if I'm out of the kitchen for too long." He washed his hands at the sink and grabbed the towel off her shoulder. "Give me a job."

Ruth nodded to the jars on the counter. "You can rough chop those if you want."

"Separate or together?"

She sighed. "I was just debating that. Let's go separate for today."

Jonah popped an olive in his mouth, his eyebrows lifting. "These are good. Where'd you find them?"

"There's a little gourmet market in town. I wasn't expecting it, either. But they have some good stuff, better than the big chain."

He nodded, still chewing. "Have any garlic?"

"Please. Do you know me at all?"

Jonah chuckled and opened the pantry. "Aha."

"What are you doing with it?"

He broke the cloves off the head and popped them smartly with the flat of the knife he'd taken from the block by the stove. "Those olives need garlic. Mix them together? It'll be great."

"You're sure?" She eyed the dough and gave it a few more kneads before shaping it back into a ball and dropping it into her oiled bowl. She flipped the dough around in the bowl so it was coated and set it at the back of the counter before draping it with the towel.

"Here." Jonah took chunks of olive and garlic and offered them to her.

Ruth popped them into her mouth and lifted her eyebrows as she chewed. "I should know better than to doubt you. Remind me why you don't go to culinary school."

His hands stilled. After a moment, he set down the knife and sighed. "I don't know. I was learning everything I thought I needed, working my way up on the job. But I didn't actually get vacation to come out here. They fired me."

Her stomach dropped into her shoes. "What? Why?"

Jonah shrugged. "New owners, new management. They have their own staff—people they've worked with for years—that they're bringing in. They'd said at first it was likely we could all keep our jobs. But I guess they changed their minds."

"What are you going to do?"

Jonah picked up the knife again and started chopping. "I was actually thinking I might move out here and keep you company. If you could use the help?"

Ruth watched her brother. He didn't look up, his gaze fixed on the olives and garlic. Maybe that was a knife safety thing but...it wasn't like him. Did he actually think she'd say no? "Even if I couldn't, I'd want you here. You're sure though? What about your friends? Melissa?"

"Melissa and I aren't...we haven't been together for a while. Since before you left, actually. Most of our friends seem to have gone with her. I didn't know how to mention it, so I didn't."

"I'm sorry. Except...kind of not. 'Cause breakfast around here just got a lot yummier. I've been making do with simple things like pancakes and scrambled eggs. But I'm guessing you can fancy us up quite a bit."

He scoffed. "If you want me to, sure. But I'm also happy to be a general helper. I know how to scrub a toilet."

"Please. Why would I keep making breakfast when I have you here? I bet we start getting guests simply for the food."

"We'll see." He set down the knife and wiped his hands.

"Thanks. I...I don't want you to do this if it's going to make things harder for you, or out of some kind of obligation."

"When have I ever?" If anything, she was more likely to refuse help even when she needed it. That was part of what happened to the first inn she'd run. It had contributed to the failure. She wasn't going to let this one fail.

8

Corban ran a hand down his cobalt blue tie. Was he too fancy? His mother had always said there was no such thing but...he was a farmer and much more comfortable in jeans and t-shirts than khakis and a tie. And yet, this mattered. Ruth mattered. She shouldn't. Not at this early stage in the game. But the fact remained that she did. Dad had always told Corban he'd know when he found the right woman. "Turns out, you were right, Dad. As usual."

His heart constricted. Would he ever stop missing them? How many times did he pick up the phone only to have to set it back down and fight back tears? Manly tears, of course. But tears, nonetheless. He swallowed the lump in his throat and forced a smile as he pushed open the door of his truck.

The bushes out front were settling in to their trimming, new buds were popping up along the cut edges. The tulips and crocuses he'd spent hours digging in with his mom were just starting to nose greenery out of the earth. When everything bloomed, the front gardens were a jumble of color. His mother had called it noisy, but he liked the carefree disorganization of it. It was a contrast to the straight, even rows that crops demanded.

He raised a hand and knocked on the front door of the B&B. Should he just walk in? Did the guests knock? Or ring the bell? Was there a protocol he should know?

"Hey, man, looking fancy." Micah tugged open the door and waggled his eyebrows. "Did Ruth know you were wearing a tie?"

Corban hunched his shoulders. "I'm not sure I mentioned that. I can take it off, if I'm overdressed."

Micah slapped him on the shoulder. "I'm just giving you a hard time. You're fine. If I know my sister—and I do—she's in a dress. She loves to get all polished up. Come on in. The other thing I know about her? She's always at least five minutes late."

"Okay." Corban tucked his hands in his pockets as he looked around the foyer. "How's it going?"

"Good. Two new couples checked in yesterday, so we're stuffed to the gunnels. But Jonah took over breakfast, so we're feasting like kings. I scrubbed toilets today for the first time in awhile. So that was fun."

Corban snickered. "You have a roommate who does yours at home or something?"

Micah shrugged. "Nope. I mostly don't bother. I give everything a good scrub couple of times a year. Figure that's enough. It's not like I'm bringing people over."

Malachi wandered into the foyer at the tail end of his brother's speech and rolled his eyes. He tapped Micah on the shoulder and signed quickly.

Micah snorted. "It's not that bad."

Corban cocked his head to the side. "What's not that bad?"

"Mal here says that my bathroom's only lacking a soul or it could stand in as roommate with a nasty personality."

"Nice one." Corban shook his head. Maybe he had missed out on something by not having siblings. The four Baxters, at least, seemed to be good friends as well as relatives. He was about to speak when Ruth came down the hall. His breath caught in his lungs. The deep purple knit dress clung to her curves in all the right places. It was an alluring combination of modest and enticing.

She finished putting in her earring and looked up, a shy smile forming on her lips. "Hi."

"Hi. You look amazing."

Malachi jammed his elbow into Micah's side and jerked his head toward the kitchen.

"You two kids have fun. We'll hold the fort. Jonah said something about a new dessert bread he was playing with this afternoon. We'll try to save you a slice." Micah grinned and turned to Malachi, his hands moving as they began a silent conversation.

"Thanks. You look...I wasn't expecting a tie."

"Is it too much?" He stroked the tie as butterflies took flight in his stomach.

"No." She reached out and touched his hand. "It's nice."

He offered his elbow. "Shall we?"

"Absolutely." She cast a look over her shoulder, visibly straightened, and turned back, a smile on her face.

"Nervous about leaving the B&B in their hands?" Corban held the door.

"No. Well. Maybe a little. But they'll be fine. The two newlywed couples are both out to eat in Twin Falls. One said something about the Magic Valley Symphony. The other...I can't recall what their plans were. But they'll be out late. And they have a key to the front door as well as a room key. Jaden's up in her room, last I noticed. I don't know what she does up there. I'll be glad when she leaves. Is that terrible?"

Corban shut the passenger door of the truck and rounded the hood. He slid onto his seat and snapped on his seatbelt. "No. I don't think so. From everything you've told me—and the little I've observed, she's odd. And there's something off about her being here."

"Having the guys here has helped. And the new guests, honestly. I don't feel like I have to look over my shoulder all the time. You know?"

"I do. I like your brothers."

She grinned. "They're pretty great, aren't they? When they're not annoying me, at least."

"I think the annoying is only because they love you. 'Cause that comes off them in waves. You're lucky to have family like that."

"I am. Having them when mom and dad died made it so much easier. Still hard, mind you, but I wasn't alone." She winced. "Sorry, that came out—"

"No, I know what you mean." He reached over and took her hand in his. He tried to ignore the warmth that settled over him at the contact. "Almost there."

Ruth's eyebrows shot up as he turned into the parking lot of what looked like a small bungalow. "This is a restaurant?"

Corban nodded to the elegant sign in the lawn. "L'Aubergine, which is supposed to sound French and fancy, but most of us mangle it pretty badly, came to town two, three years ago? No one understood why they didn't find a place in Twin Falls. We're used to driving into the city if we want something upscale. But this is where they wanted to be. I'm not sure they're doing more than struggling along, but they source local and the things they do with their food. I've been known to come by myself now and again when I'm in the mood for something a little different than what I can whip up."

"I can't wait."

He smiled and gave his name to the hostess who led them immediately through the first room where a few parties were already seated and into the mostly-empty second. She seated them at a small table in the corner by a bay window that looked out on a back garden.

"This is lovely. And so clever, to keep most of the original footprint of the house and make separate dining rooms like this. It makes it cozy."

Intimate. That's the word Corban would have used. The lights in the room were dim, and the candlelight intensified the romantic atmosphere. Was this too much for a first date? Or third, depending on how you counted. He swallowed and dragged his attention back to Ruth, who had continued talking. What had he missed? The food. She'd been asking about the menu. "I don't think you can go wrong, no matter what you choose."

She smiled and flipped the leather folder closed. "Then I'm set."

"That was fast." He looked down at the menu, his mouth watering as he read the options. "What are you getting?"

"The special with local sausages."

He nodded. Nico Delis made good sausage. It was nice to see another local restaurant picking up on that. "Good choice. Just made my decision easier."

The server appeared and filled their water glasses. She took drink orders and, when Corban mentioned they were ready, their food as well.

"Quick. And quiet. I never heard her coming."

Corban chuckled. "I think they give them special stealth shoes."

She laughed and his heart lifted.

What a sound. He didn't want it to ever end. "I could've used those growing up when I was trying to spy on my brothers."

"Can I ask you a question?"

"Of course."

"Has Malachi...I mean, when did he..."

"His hearing?"

Corban nodded. "I wasn't sure if it was insensitive to ask. But you all seem so comfortable signing, I wondered."

"He was in an accident when he was five. He had a major head injury and for the longest time they worried he'd have brain damage, but when all was said and done, he just lost his hearing. They tried an implant, but it didn't help enough for him to think it was worth the obvious equipment. It made him so self-conscious. I've often wondered if he'd try again now that he's older, but I don't ask. I figure he's happy, so why push."

"Is it hard to learn sign language?"

"I guess that depends on how good you are at learning languages. It's a lot like any foreign language. You just need to practice."

There were probably books at the library. He'd go look. Seemed like it would be worth doing. Malachi was an interesting guy.

"He reads lips really well. It's not like you need to sign."

"I get that. But it seems reasonable that you learn to talk with your friends."

Ruth smiled. "Well, if you want to practice, let me know."

CORBAN TURNED off the engine and turned. "I had a really nice time. Thanks for coming out with me."

"Thanks for asking." Ruth looked at the B&B and sighed. "Guess I should get in there and make sure nothing happened."

"I'm sure they would've called." He undid his seatbelt. "I'll walk you up."

"You don't have to."

He shook his head and hopped out of the truck, hurrying around to get her door before she could get out. He took her hand in his and gave a light squeeze. "It's my pleasure."

At the front door, she stopped and turned. "Thanks again."

"Can we do it again sometime? I'm not sure what your schedule is like, and things are starting to get busy, but I want to see you again."

"I'd like that." Ruth hesitated a moment before rising on her tiptoes and brushing her lips across his cheek. "Good night, Corban."

"'Night." He swallowed, fighting the urge to grab her and kiss her back. It was too soon. Much too soon. He waited until she'd stepped into the foyer before turning to head back to his truck. She was still standing in the doorway when he climbed into the cab. He smiled and lifted a hand before cranking the engine.

Lord? Thank You. That was the best date I've had in...ever. I have to think You had something to do with it, with bringing Ruth here. Guide me—us—in our relationship. Let it always honor You...don't let me rush things.

9

Ruth waved goodbye to the nice, older couple as they drove away. She'd been here almost a full month and things were finally settling into place. Her brothers had left after a week, but Jonah would be back tomorrow with all his stuff. How he'd tied everything up in only two weeks she couldn't fathom, but at least he hadn't hit any major snags. For now he'd take over the smallest of the rooms upstairs, but they'd have to figure something out that could be more permanent. He'd sold as much as he could, but some would stay in storage. That was an expense neither of them were excited about.

But as of now, she had an empty B&B and plans for a quiet evening with Corban, Emerson, and Pam. They'd done a few things together, when they could find time—or make it. That was more honest. It didn't matter what she had planned, when Corban called, Ruth did what she could to make it work. Being with him was the most settled she'd felt in years. It was a quiet, comfortable friendship that held the promise of more.

She hoped that more might happen sooner than later, but the man seemed to have the patience of Job. In this case, it wasn't an admirable trait.

Ruth cut thick slices from a cinnamon raisin loaf she'd baked that morning and arranged them on a tray. She eyed the olive and garlic loaf and shrugged. Why not? They'd probably order something in, but bread and some cheese never went amiss. In fact...she crossed to the fridge and pulled it open. She had some sliced meat and leftover olives. There was enough for a good antipasto tray. With the bread, they might not need to order something after all.

Humming quietly, Ruth arranged meat, cheese, olives, sun-dried tomatoes, and artichoke hearts on a plate. Those artichoke hearts...it had seemed like a good idea, but there was simply too much moisture in them to put them in bread. There had to be a way. Maybe Jonah would have an idea. She'd run into that a couple of times now. Some things just couldn't go in bread without leaving it soggy in the middle despite the slight char on the crust.

She mixed a small bowl of olive oil and some fragrant herbs for dipping—the olive bread in particular was delightful that way. Plain sourdough worked well, too. For the cinnamon raisin...she was out of cream cheese, but butter would be fine. She'd put together some honey butter at breakfast and there was enough left that they should be fine.

"Knock, knock." Corban stepped through the kitchen door, his gaze traveling to the food on the counter. "That looks good. Not in the mood for Chinese?"

"Not really. Is that okay? I mean, the three of you can still order if you want." Ruth chewed her lower lip. "Or I can put this away. I wasn't trying to be rude."

"No, it looks great." He crossed the distance and slipped his arms around her, pulling her close. "Hi."

Ruth encircled his waist with her arms, warmth and peace stealing through her. "Hi back. I'm glad I don't have guests tonight. This is just what I needed."

"An evening with friends?"

She tilted her head up and met his gaze. "That too."

One corner of his mouth quirked up and he lowered his forehead to hers. "Ruth?"

Her heart started racing. Was he finally going to kiss her? "Yes?"

"May I?" His voice was quiet, his gaze fixed on hers.

"Please."

His lips lowered to hers and her eyes drifted closed. Her fingers clenched at his waist as she lost herself in the sensation of kissing Corban DeWitt.

"Hey guys. Oh. Sorry. The front door was open so we just...we'll be in the lounge." Emerson cleared his throat.

Corban eased back, shaking his head. "He never had very good timing."

Heat burned Ruth's cheeks.

"Hey." Corban brushed his thumb along her cheekbone. "Come on, let's take the food out. Seeing as how Em and Pam have two kids, I'm guessing they've kissed once or twice."

She snickered, the need for the floor to open and swallow her whole dissipating. "All right."

Corban took the tray of meat and the bowl of oil. Ruth picked up the bread and butter. They could figure out drinks later. And maybe Pam and Emerson would want to order in anyway.

"So. My husband has great timing as usual. Sorry about that." Pam's eyes danced with mirth as Ruth set the tray down on the coffee table in the middle of the seating area. "But I can't say I'm upset to know things are moving along between the two of you. You're such a good pair."

"Thanks." Ruth crossed her arms. "Drinks? I have iced tea and lemonade. Or water, of course. Or I can make a pot of coffee?"

"Iced tea is good." Emerson plucked an olive from the tray and popped it in his mouth. "Mmm. These are good. Where'd you find them?"

"Benita's? It's a little market in the Arcadia Shopping Center. They have some fancier things that you can't get at the grocery store. And more varieties of health food type things if you're into that." Ruth wrinkled her nose. She skipped those aisles. Deliberately.

"Let me help you get the tea." Pam stood and followed Ruth into the kitchen. "I'm really sorry. We didn't mean to embarrass you."

"It's okay." Her cheeks were on fire again.

Pam frowned. "That wasn't your first kiss?"

Ruth cleared her throat and opened the cupboard where she kept the glasses.

"Oh. I'm so sorry. I'll kick Emerson later, if you want?"

"Don't do that. It's fine. I just hope Corban will want to do it again sometime before I'm ninety."

Pam laughed. "He was always a slow mover. But now that he's started, it shouldn't be as bad. I think it's just inertia."

"Inertia? Really?"

Pam shrugged. "What else would you call it?"

"I don't know. Something that I haven't forgotten from high school physics."

"Doesn't sound like you've forgotten it if you know it's from physics."

"True enough." Ruth took a deep breath. Time to change the subject. "Why don't you grab the pitcher out of the fridge? And if you guys had your heart set on Chinese, we can still do that."

Pam groaned and started back to the sitting room. "I was racking my brain the whole way over here for another alternative. We've had Chinese the past couple shifts and I'm over it."

"I generally feel that way. I mean, I'll eat it if it's what everyone wants, but it's never been a favorite."

"What's not a favorite?" Emerson looked up from buttering a slice of bread.

"She's tired of Chinese, too." Pam set the glasses down. "Thus this amazing spread. Did you make the bread again?"

Ruth nodded.

"Can I buy a loaf from you sometime? The girls on the unit would go nuts for this." Pam took a slice of olive bread and ripped off a piece before dunking it in the seasoned oil.

Buy a loaf? That wasn't...she wasn't...Ruth shook her head. "I'll give you one. I have an extra in the kitchen. Remind me before you leave."

"What have you guys been up to?" Corban reached for a slice of salami and wrapped it together with a slice of cheddar.

Emerson leaned back, crossing his feet at the ankles. "We went to help start up a community garden, couple of Saturdays back. The boys loved that. There were a handful of other kids their age—kids of all ages, actually. The boys and I've been back a few times to check on the progress of the seedlings and just look around."

"How'd you hear about that?" Ruth took a slice of olive bread.

"There were flyers around town. It's on the old Akers Garden Center lot, near the church, actually." Emerson frowned as he studied the trays of food and selected another snack. "I hope they keep it going. A community garden is a great thing. I know the boys and I would enjoy doing more over there."

"I like the Akers Garden folks. I've set up a standing order for some arrangements for the B&B from their flower shop. There's nothing like fresh flowers to brighten a space." Ruth nodded to the colorful bouquet arranged in a cut-glass vase on the sideboard. "They've been great to work with."

"I like flowers." Pam sent Emerson a significant look.

He winced. "I should take the boys by sometime and see what they have."

"Yes. You should." Pam smiled and patted his knee then turned to Ruth. "Corban says one of your brothers is moving out here as well?"

Ruth smiled, nodding. "Jonah. He gets here tomorrow. I can't wait. Not only is he fun to have around, he's an amazing chef. He's taking over breakfast and I'm over the moon. He may end up looking for another position, too. Maybe at L'Aubergine. That's the sort of thing he did in D.C. I guess we'll see what happens."

The evening continued with stories from Emerson about homeschooling the boys and Pam's tales from the surgical unit. Corban seemed content to listen, chiming in here and there, but not as much as he usually did. Ruth caught his eye a few times, and he'd smile and give her hand a squeeze but...was something wrong?

When the grandfather clock in the foyer chimed half-past-nine, Pam sighed. "We should get going. My parents won't put the boys to bed, so they're already up too late. But if they're up much later they won't go to sleep for hours, they get wound up when they're tired."

Emerson stood and offered a hand to his wife. "Thanks for having us over. This was fun. Maybe some time the two of you can come see the house. We're almost settled."

Pam scoffed. "Don't listen to him. We haven't even been in there a week. Next month, though, consider yourself invited."

Ruth and Corban followed them to the front door and waved as they walked to their car. When they'd left, Ruth shut the front door and turned to the lounge. She'd put the food away and leave the dishes in the sink for tomorrow. With no guests, she had a little extra leeway.

Corban put a hand on her shoulder and swung her back to face him.

Ruth met his gaze. "Everything okay?"

He smiled and drew her close, his mouth lowering to hers. "It will be."

10

C orban stopped the tractor and looked across the road. He hadn't planned to be out here today. The planting was moving along well enough that he didn't need to work. But he hadn't wanted to sit around inside, either. He'd taken a little walk around the property near the house. He'd even wandered into the little garden his mother used to love. Its picket fence needed some repair and another coat of paint. The waterfall wasn't working—probably needed a new pump. Most of the plants were dead, and their beds filled with weeds. Except for the rose bushes that just needed a good pruning. He'd added it to his list of things to do, but it brought too many memories to tackle today. So he'd gone ahead and gotten out the tractor. Spock was still enjoying running around, chasing rabbits...or the rabbits that lived in his imagination, at least. So he might as well get something done while he let the dog play. And if it let him get a look across at Ruth, well then, that was even better. Right?

As if he'd conjured her with his thoughts, Ruth stepped out of the front door. She paused on the steps and shaded her eyes, then lifted her arm and waved wildly. Skipping down the last two steps, she jogged to the road, and scarcely glanced both ways before darting across.

"I was hoping I'd see you."

Corban grinned. "That's always nice to hear. What's up?"

"I'm on my way in to Twin Falls to pick up Jonah. Wondered if you might want to tag along, but it looks like you're busy? We could grab dinner in town, or picnic somewhere?"

A picnic would be fun. "Have you been to Shoshone Falls yet?"

Ruth shook her head.

"It's a nice place to picnic. And a good place to stretch your legs after a long flight, so your brother will probably enjoy it, too. You sure he won't mind if I'm along?" He didn't need Jonah getting annoyed about their relationship. As the oldest of the boys, did Jonah feel some kind of paternal responsibility? Would Corban pass muster?

"He suggested it." She checked her watch. "Why don't I go put a picnic together—I probably have enough in the fridge to make something good—and then I'll swing by and pick you up. Maybe fifteen minutes?"

That'd give him time to get the tractor put away and maybe hurry through the shower, get some of the dust off. He nodded. "Sounds good."

"'K. See you in a few." Ruth dashed back across the road.

Corban watched until she was back inside, then, with a sharp whistle for Spock, he started the tractor and turned back toward the farmhouse.

"HERE WE ARE." Corban pointed to the turn. He dug into his pocket for his wallet and pulled out three singles. "You might need this."

Ruth frowned. "I can—"

"Please. I'm happy to do it, if they're collecting. Call it a welcome-to-Idaho present for Jonah."

"Oh no. Leave me out of it. Though I don't happen to have three bucks on me right now, so I'm also not offering to pay." Jonah leaned forward and peeked between the front seats. "But someone should pay so we can go in. Whatever's in that cooler in the trunk smells good. And I'm hungry. The bag of chips I grabbed in Salt Lake City on my layover was a long time ago."

Ruth sighed and took the bills. "Thank you."

Corban grinned. "You're welcome. Park right over there."

She navigated to an empty parking spot and turned off the engine. "Everyone hungry?"

"Let's wait a minute. We should walk out, see the falls. There ought to actually be water this time of year. They regulate the flow, so the experience isn't always what you expect based on the website." Corban pushed open the door and stood. He breathed in deeply, there was nothing like the air by the falls. He walked around the car and caught the door as Ruth pushed it open. He took her hand as she stood and squeezed.

"Coming, Jonah?" Ruth turned.

"Yeah, just trying to extract myself from this backseat. Is it possible to have less leg room in a sedan? 'Cause I'm not sure how." Jonah wiggled out of the car and stretched. "Ugh. That's worse than the plane."

"This way." Corban tugged Ruth's hand and onto the path that led to the falls. They reached the viewpoint easily. Water gushed into the river below and, as always, Corban's thoughts strayed to the insignificance of man when faced with the God who could create something so magnificent with just a word.

"It's magnificent. Why haven't I made time to get down here before now? I've barely left the B&B. I certainly haven't been into the city, for all I've sent my guests down here." Ruth leaned her head against Corban's arm with a little sigh. "I'm glad you thought of this."

He pressed a kiss to the top of her head and slid his arm around her shoulders. "Don't beat yourself up. You've been busy. I imagine if you hadn't had a surprise guest your second full week you might have gotten out."

"Most likely. But since I didn't, I get to see it with you. That's even better."

"Are we going to eat?" Jonah stepped next to Ruth and crossed his arms. "I'm getting hungry."

Ruth chuckled and fished in her pocket. Her hand emerged with the car keys and she offered them to her brother. "Go get the cooler out of the trunk and set up a spot. We'll be there in a few."

He took the keys, grumbling under his breath, and headed back up to the grassy spot.

"I should go help..."

"No. You should kiss me."

He flashed a grin. "Should I? Well, I wouldn't want to disappoint anyone."

CORBAN PULLED his truck into the driveway of the B&B and frowned. Why was there a "For Sale" sign in the yard? Ruth hadn't mentioned anything about leaving. And Jonah had moved in two weeks ago. It didn't make any sense. He tapped the real estate agent name into his phone as he strode to the front door. It wasn't a familiar name.

"Oh, thank goodness you're here." Ruth ran a hand through her hair, leaving a thin trail of flour. "Do you think you can get that thing out of my yard? I've been on the phone with the real estate agent's office all morning and can't get a straight answer about how it came to be there."

"That's a relief." The vague thoughts of begging her to stay could be put on hold. At least for a while. He already found himself browsing online jewelry stores with disturbing regularity. It was ridiculous to look at engagement rings when he hadn't even said "I love you" yet. Neither of them had. "I'll go see what I can do."

Corban strode to the sign and gave it a shake. There was a little movement. He tucked his phone into his back pocket and set to work wiggling the post back and forth until it loosened enough for him to tug from the ground. He tossed it aside and tamped the earth back in place. The grass would grow over it eventually.

"Can you take it around back? Maybe lean it on the far side of the shed?" Ruth stood on the front stoop, her arms crossed.

"Sure thing."

"Thanks. Come on in the kitchen door when you're done. I just finished a new tea bread and need a taste-tester."

Tea bread? He hefted the sign up onto his shoulder and started around the house. How was that different from bread? Though the concoctions Ruth put together surpassed anything he'd ever called bread before. Maybe they all had fancy names, too. They were delicious. That's all that mattered to him.

He dropped the sign beside the shed and dusted off his clothes. He'd showered and changed after being in the fields all morning. So much for looking nicer than he usually managed.

"Thank you, Corban." Ruth wrapped her arms around his waist as he stepped into the kitchen. "I'm so mad. I yelled at some poor woman who had the misfortune to answer the phone at the real estate agent's. They're looking into it and will get back to me. Who would do this?"

"I don't know. But we'll get it figured out." He rubbed her

back. Would it soothe her? He'd never seen her this upset. He kissed her forehead. "Where's Jonah?"

She nestled her head on his shoulder. "He volunteered to take the couple we have staying here into Twin Falls. They didn't rent a car—I guess they thought we were closer to town than we are. I think he was going to go ziplining while he waited for them to do their rafting trip, even if it meant a little driving back and forth through town. I spent the morning cleaning, and when I came down to start in the kitchen, saw the sign, and I've been on the phone, or waiting for calls, since. Thus the tea bread. Oh. Let me get you a slice. Sit down."

Chuckling under his breath, he sat while Ruth bustled around. "Be honest, okay? You don't have to like it."

"I'm sure I will." Corban sniffed the slice of bread before taking a giant bite. His eyes watered as he chewed. "It's...interesting. Can I have some water?"

"It's too much, isn't it?" Ruth sighed as she crossed to the tap to fill a glass. "I got distracted and I think I added cloves three times. I was hoping maybe it was just me and it would be okay."

Corban drained the glass and cleared his throat. What was he supposed to say?

Ruth laughed. "I can see the wheels turning. You don't have to say it."

"What was it supposed to be?"

"Orange bread, with some clove to spice it up a little. But a little goes a long way with cloves. As you can see." She took the plate and carried it to the sink. She dumped the rest of the slice in the trash and set the plate on the counter. "Would you like something else? I have all the usuals."

"I'm good. I don't always come over to eat. I just wanted to see you. It's been a busy morning, uncovering all the early plants. Now that we're into May, it should be safe enough. Planted the last field. So it's just a matter of making sure everything's coming along. Lettuce and spinach will be ready to pick in June, but nothing else until July. That's when things will keep me hopping." Corban held out his hand and waited until she crossed the kitchen and sat back down, her fingers curving around his. "Ruth? I wanted to tell—"

The phone rang and Ruth popped out of her seat, darting across the room to grab the handset from its base. "I'm so sorry. Hold that thought." She pushed a button on the phone. "Fairview B&B, this is Ruth."

Corban's shoulders slumped. He'd been working up the courage to tell her he loved her for a week now. The timing never seemed right. Was God trying to tell him something?

"Uh huh. Yes, I have it. Thanks." Ruth hung up the phone and frowned. "Well, it seems the sign was stolen several weeks ago from a property in Twin Falls that just went on the market. The police are working on it."

"Now what?"

"I guess I call the detective in charge and see what there is to see. Which is not what I need to be doing."

Corban drummed his fingers on the table. "Want to call Emerson instead? Have him look into it?"

"I don't know. I don't want to impose on him."

He shrugged. "Seems like this might be a situation where having an attorney might make a conversation go faster. I can't see how it would hurt to have your attorney also be a friend."

"Okay. That makes sense. Will you call him?"

"Of course." Corban dug out his cell phone and punched Emerson's number. "Hey, Em. Got a sec? Cool."

He explained the situation as clearly as he could and waited while Emerson asked some questions that neither he nor Ruth had answers to. "Sure. See you in a few."

"He's coming here?"

Corban nodded. "He thought it'd be easier to make the call

from here, with you by him in case there were more questions. I'll take the boys out in the back yard so they can run around, and that way you won't be disturbed."

"You don't have to do that. I can put the TV on in the lounge. I'd like you here. Is that okay?" She slid her arm around his waist.

Warmth worked its way through him. "If that's what you want, then that's what I'll do."

11

R uth paced the kitchen. She needed to be doing something. Waiting was driving her crazy.

"Come here." Corban held out a hand. "Why don't we pray? Pacing isn't going to get us anywhere."

She blew out a breath. That was a good idea. Sort of. Did God really care about her? When she'd found out about the B&B it had seemed like He might—even if He'd taken Naomi in order to show it. Seemed like there was nothing good that didn't have some hint of sorrow attached to it. But now? Was she going to lose everything? Was it going to be more proof that anything she touched turned to dust? Ruth crossed to the kitchen table and sat, folding her hands in her lap.

Corban picked up her hands and wrapped them between his. It was a comforting gesture that left her insides gooey. This man. He was special. And she never would have met him if she hadn't come here. But if the B&B...no. She wouldn't go there just yet.

He squeezed her hands before starting to speak. "Heavenly Father, we're coming to You now a little bit confused and worried. We don't have much information yet, but we also know

You're in control. We're trusting You with the B&B, and with our future. Jesus, it feels like everything is connected and I know that as much as Ruth doesn't want to lose this place now that she's making it her own, I don't want to lose the woman I love. Thank You for bringing her to Arcadia Valley and to me. Hold us in the palm of Your hand and give us peace. Amen."

Ruth opened her eyes and sought his gaze. He loved her?

"I knocked, but no one answered, so I just came in. I hope that's okay?" Emerson poked his head into the kitchen.

"Where are the boys?" Ruth dragged her spinning thoughts back to the present. She could worry about whether or not Corban loved her later. "I have some DVDs..."

"I dropped them by my parents. I wasn't sure how long this would take and figured that was safer. Dad was saying they might walk down to the community garden greenhouses and check on the seedlings. I can't imagine there's much to see yet, but the kids were excited by the prospect. I'm guessing there'll be ice cream involved, too." Emerson stuck his hands in his pockets. "Why don't you fill me in?"

"Let's move into the lounge. Do you want a drink or snack?" Ruth pulled her hands from Corban's and stood.

"I'm fine. Thanks."

Corban held her gaze for a moment before he stood and followed Emerson out of the kitchen. Ruth pressed a hand to her stomach and took a deep breath. *God? If You're going to help, I'd really love it if it was now.*

RUTH FOCUSED all her attention on pulling the strudel dough as thin as she could without tearing. It was the only thing she'd been able to think of that would force her not to stress about anything after Emerson and Corban left. She hadn't made strudel in a long time. She'd learned when she was younger, working with her grandmother in the kitchen while the boys ran wild on their California farm during the annual summer trip west. Most people cheated and used store made phyllo, but it wasn't the same. Still, the temptation was reasonable. Stretching dough using only your knuckles was slow and tedious.

Jonah clomped into the kitchen and stopped. "What's wrong?"

"What do you mean?" Ruth didn't look up as she worked her hands from the center of the square out.

"You're making strudel. You only make strudel when you don't want to think. You only don't want to think when something's wrong." Jonah crossed to the sink and washed his hands. He moved to the other side of the island, slid his hands under the pastry, and began pulling in the opposite direction.

"Careful." Ruth frowned. Two people could make it go faster. But it could also result in huge holes.

"I know. Now tell me."

She sighed and began to pour out the story, from the sign in the yard forward. "So, Emerson talked to the detective, who had basically chalked the whole thing up to kids. The neighbor of the original house where the sign was got a cell phone photo of the person stealing the sign, which the police forwarded to Emerson. It was Jaden. So I called her and she referred me to her attorney. She's contesting the will. And in the mean time, I guess, trying to get me to give up and leave. Or something. Emerson thinks it's an attempt to circumvent the entire process. He says contesting a will in court rarely changes the outcome— you have to work very hard to prove undue influence and her chances are effectively nil. But even though there's very little chance that she'll win, she can tie things up in court for a long time."

"Oh man."

Ruth nodded. Court meant money. Money she didn't have. She blinked back tears. "It's happening again."

"No. No, it isn't. Not necessarily." Jonah slid his hands out from under the dough and came around the island to wrap Ruth in his arms. "This is nothing like Rosemont. There's no preppy snob taking you out to try and steal your secrets in order to give the inside scoop to a third party. And you're not trying to go this alone. Two major factors in the first disaster."

"But it's still me, Jonah. Everything I touch falls apart." She buried her head in his shoulder, the words echoing in her ears. A small, quiet voice in her head yelled that they weren't true. But the slideshow of her experiences in life drowned it out. It's why she'd given up after the Rosemont and gone from one retail job to another. What was the point in having dreams when chasing them always ended so badly? "Besides, Corban..."

"Is an honest man who, if I can read people at all, is at least half in love with you. Don't try to lump him in with Lars. I mean really, Lars? Who names their kid that?"

Probably a ton of Swedish people. But that wasn't the point. Was Corban half in love? All the way? Either one, he hadn't said it to her. Not really. Did she want him to? She did. So, so much. She couldn't be the one to say it first this time. Couldn't— wouldn't—risk that. But Jonah was right. Corban was nothing like Lars. She sniffled. "What am I going to do?"

Jonah stepped back and gave her shoulder an awkward pat. "What did Emerson say?"

Ruth wiped her eyes on her shoulder and looked down at the pastry. It was ready. She took the small pan of melted butter off the stove and dug a brush out of a drawer. "He said he needed to look into some things and he'd call me later tonight. Or email. And until then he said not to worry."

He chuckled. "Thus the strudel."

"It was all I could think of." She brushed the butter over the paper-thin dough. "Grab the bowl of filling from the fridge, would you?"

Jonah took a large bowl out and waited for her to set aside the butter. "I know it's hard, but let's try to take his advice. At least the not worrying part. He's a lawyer too, you said, right?"

Ruth nodded and took the bowl. She spread the chopped apples, raisins, and nuts coated in a cinnamon, sugar, and flour mixture across the pastry. Setting aside the bowl, she moved to the short end of the rectangle and began the slow, careful process of rolling the concoction.

"So we'll wait. And eat strudel." He grinned and stepped out of the way.

"Grab the sheet tray?"

This was the tricky part, getting the thick roll onto the baking tray without ripping any of the layers. Or dropping it. She wiggled one long piece onto the tray, then, holding her breath, flipped the other up and into a large horseshoe.

"Nice. Any butter left?"

"Of course." She retrieved the pan and brushed butter across the top and down the sides. "The oven should be ready. Thanks, Jonah."

"Hey. That's what I'm here for."

12

Corban idly scrubbed Spock's head with one hand while he rocked on the front porch. His Bible was open in his lap, but he stared out into the darkening front yard, mulling over the words he'd just read. He'd always struggled with injustice, and the goings on with Ruth today screamed of that. Why was it that evil sometimes prospered? It was the question of the ages, apparently. And the reminder from Psalm 37 to not fret over the one who prospers from evil was timely. Even if he couldn't quite reconcile that with wanting to defend Ruth. Seeing the hurt and fear in her eyes had nearly undone him.

He loved her.

The words had slipped out in his prayer. Had she caught them? If Emerson hadn't shown up...well, he had. So that was a moot point. But now what? Was she ready to hear it? Was he ready to say it aloud, for real? He wasn't a kid anymore. If only she'd come before his parents passed. How they would've loved her.

Headlights turned into the drive. Corban frowned. "Looks like we've got some company, Spock."

Jonah stepped down from the truck and lifted a hand.

"Evening." Corban grinned as Spock trotted down the steps barking and circling around the new arrival.

"Hey. Hope it's okay. I thought about calling...but I didn't want Ruth to know I was coming over."

Corban's eyebrows lifted. That seemed unusual. "Oh?"

"I brought you some strudel."

"Where'd you get strudel?" Corban's mouth watered. Mrs. Mauz, their neighbor when he was a kid, had made the world's most incredible strudel. When she'd died and their farm was sold, he'd given up looking for the treat. No one did it like she did.

"Ruth made it. She only does it when she's trying not to think too hard. It's a pain."

Homemade? It had to be better than the soggy mess the stores—and even the bakery in town—tried to pass off. "Come on in. You bring enough for two?"

"Do I look dumb?" Jonah laughed and held up the container. "Whose truck?"

"Mine." Jonah pulled open the screen door and followed Corban to the kitchen. "I sold my car before moving out—seemed easier all around. I saw this one online last night, checked into it today when I took the couple staying at the B&B into town. It wasn't hard to convince them to drive Ruth's car back. They'd planned to get a rental—still might—but you can tell they don't want to."

"When do they leave?" Corban pulled down two plates and got out glasses. "Milk?"

Jonah nodded. "Day after tomorrow? The one after that? Sometime soon. They can probably do without. Ruth's a soft touch."

Corban sat and offered Jonah a knife. "You want to do the honors?"

"Sure." Jonah tugged the foil off the container and sliced the hunk of strudel in half. He slid the pieces onto the plates and pushed one toward Corban. "Emerson called."

"I wondered if that might be why you came." He battled disappointment that Ruth hadn't picked up the phone or come herself. Though she had guests. Maybe she couldn't get away. Or maybe she didn't feel the way he did.

"I'm sure Ruth'll call you tonight, after everyone heads up to bed. This couple likes to sit and chat in the lounge. That wasn't really why I came. I—" He took a deep breath and stabbed up a bite of apples. "Has she told you much about her first inn?"

Corban shook his head. He hadn't pried. "I figured she'd tell me when she wanted to."

Jonah scoffed and pointed his fork at Corban's plate. "You have to at least try it."

Corban poked his fork into the pastry, the flaky layers giving way and exposing glistening apples. It looked like a strudel should. Putting the bite in his mouth, he closed his eyes.

"Good, right?" Jonah grinned. "Anyway. The Rosemont— that was her first inn—it was a disaster, almost from day one. There was a bigger company interested in the property, couldn't get the owners to sell to them...long story short, they ended up forcing Ruth to close. She's never really recovered."

"That's horrible. But...I guess I'm not following?"

"She's worried it's happening again. And I'm worried she'll just give up, not fight. Unless she feels like there's a reason. Maybe there's something—or someone—here worth fighting for?"

Corban coughed as the apple went down the wrong way. He reached for his milk and took a long swig. "Subtlety isn't your strong suit."

Jonah shrugged.

"What are you asking?"

"Are you in this for the long haul? Or are you just playing with my sister 'cause she's new in town and something different?"

"Is forever long enough?"

Jonah held Corban's gaze for several heartbeats before a slow grin spread across his face. "Yeah. Welcome to the family, man."

"Well now, Ruth might have something to say about that. So let's not jump—"

"No conclusion jumping here. I'm pretty sure she's already completely in love with you. So barring some colossal screw up, you're set."

Corban's heart leapt. Right before it crashed back to reality. What would her brother know? Ruth didn't strike him as the kind of woman who sat and divulged her inmost thoughts and feelings to her brother. To anyone, for that matter. She kept it all so quiet. "You think?"

Jonah nodded. "Which brings me back around to why I'm here tonight."

"So it wasn't just to bring me strudel? I'm crushed."

Jonah snickered. "Nope. It's to ask you to be patient with her. This...whatever it is with the B&B is throwing her off. She'll probably try to clam up and close everyone out. Don't let her."

Corban nodded and scraped the last bits of strudel off his plate.

With a sigh, Jonah pushed back from the table. "I should probably head back before Ruth wonders where I went. See ya."

"Come by anytime. Especially if you have dessert."

Jonah laughed.

After the truck pulled out of the driveway, Corban collected his Bible from the porch and sent Spock out to do his business one final time. Should he call Emerson and get the scoop? Probably better to wait and see if Ruth got in touch. And if she didn't...he checked the time. He'd give her an hour before he called.

~

"STRUDEL?" Ruth held out a plate with a professional smile that didn't reach her eyes.

Corban frowned. He took the plate, set it on the counter, and stepped closer.

Ruth stepped back.

"Something wrong?"

"I'm just really busy. This isn't a good time."

"Ah. Your guests are still here?"

"No." She sighed. "They checked out this morning. Jonah took them to the airport."

"So you need to turn the rooms."

"No. I did that already. It's not...I'm just busy, okay? Don't you have work you should be doing?" She crossed her arms.

"I do. But I thought seeing you, making sure you were okay was more important. You didn't answer when I called last night." Corban tried to catch her gaze.

"I was—"

"Busy. Sure. I get it." Maybe Jonah was wrong. If she pushed him away this hard, shouldn't he respect her wishes? His heart ached at the thought. And yet. "Do you really want me to go?"

"It would be easier." She turned and busied herself at the sink.

He watched her attack the pan and keep scrubbing long after any hint of egg remained. "That's not what I asked."

The pan clattered into the sink and she turned, suds dripping off her hands onto the floor. "What do you want from me?"

A lifetime together. Children. He bit back the words. "An honest answer. Do you want me to go?"

Her eyes filled with tears. She gave an imperceptible shake of her head.

His breath came out in a whoosh and he closed the distance between them so he could wrap his arms around her.

"I'm all soapy. You'll get wet." She tried to step back.

Corban tightened his grip. "I don't care. I love you, Ruth."

She blinked, her breath catching, before she threw her arms around his neck, a tear slipping down her cheek. He lowered his lips to hers, reveling in the rightness of it. *I am my beloved's.* The snippet of Scripture flitted through his mind before he was lost to the kiss.

Someone cleared their throat.

Ruth jerked in his arms, her cheeks flushing as she wiggled out of his embrace.

"Sorry to interrupt."

Corban rolled his head on his neck and turned. "Uh huh."

Emerson grinned and shrugged. "I am. Mostly. But I'm also glad to see it."

"Maybe you want to go away for a little bit? Come back later?" Corban reached for Ruth's hand and pulled her to his side.

"Corban." Ruth jabbed him in the side with her elbow.

"I take it she didn't mention I was coming over to discuss strategy."

"She didn't mention it, no." Corban lifted an eyebrow.

Ruth hunched her shoulders. "I just hadn't gotten to it."

Too busy trying to get him to go away and avoiding his call. Probably not wise to say that. He hummed.

"Can I get you some strudel, Emerson? Corban was just about to have a slice. I made it yesterday. We could sit in the lounge." Ruth turned and started cutting another slice of the apple concoction.

"It's good. A lot like Mrs. Mauz used to make."

Emerson brightened. "Really? Count me in."

"How do you know it's good?" Ruth turned and offered a plate to Emerson.

Corban winced. "Jonah brought me a piece last night."

She shook her head. "I knew that chunk was more than he could eat himself. Go sit down. I'll be there in a minute."

13

R uth waited until the men left the room before she sagged against the counter and tried to calm down. There was too much going on—too many highs and lows. She simply wasn't cut out for this much drama. Corban loved her. She closed her eyes and repeated it to herself. She pressed a hand to her quivering stomach. She hadn't gotten the opportunity to tell him she loved him, too. But she would. She'd make a point of it.

She took a deep breath and straightened her shoulders. That would have to wait. With Emerson here, it was time to figure out a plan. Hopefully one that didn't involve selling the Fairview and slinking back to the D.C. area. She liked it here in Arcadia Valley. The two months she'd been her had been the first time she'd felt at home in a long time. Corban had a lot to do with that. But so did their church and the town in general. She needed to stay.

With a plate of strudel for herself, she pushed through the kitchen door and crossed into the lounge.

"This is amazing. You made this?" Emerson forked up another bite of apples.

"Yesterday. I'm glad you like it." She perched on the edge of the loveseat next to Corban. He reached over and took her hand. "So?"

Emerson cleared his throat and set the plate aside. "I did some calling around yesterday and a little more this morning. Everyone generally agrees that Jaden has no chance of winning in court if she pushes that far with her contest of the will. The best chance she has would be to prove undue influence, but that's not particularly likely given that you and Naomi have been longtime friends and there are people who can vouch for that. Frankly, I'm surprised she found an attorney who'd take her on as a client."

"Which means what?" Ruth looked down at the plate of strudel and set it aside. She could eat it later. If she ever got her appetite back.

"That's trickier. She can go on being a nuisance and take you to court. I can't tell you how long that could drag out or whether she'd find a judge willing to hear the case. Or we can try to get her to give up."

Corban furrowed his brow. "How? This all came out of nowhere. What makes you think she'd give up?"

Emerson rubbed the back of his neck. "From talking to her attorney, I get the impression that Jaden's most concerned that you're going to make a living off what her sister started."

"Now wait just a cotton-pickin' minute. Naomi took over the fully-functional B&B from my mother. She didn't start anything." Corban set his empty plate down on the coffee table a little more forcefully than necessary.

Emerson held up a hand. "I understand that. And I presented that point to Jaden's attorney this morning. It was, apparently, news to him. I get the feeling that he's starting to realize his client hasn't been particularly forthcoming in terms of the truth."

Ruth's shoulders sagged. "But I *am* trying to make a living here. You're not suggesting we close?"

Emerson nodded. "Only temporarily. Though we wouldn't tell anyone that. I believe that if Jaden thinks you're simply living in her sister's, hang on," he scrolled through notes on his phone, "ah, and I quote, 'dumb old house filled with dusty furniture' that she'd be inclined to let it go. She has a house. She has no interest in moving out here. It just appears to be the ongoing income that upsets her."

Close down. Fail. Again. She widened her eyes to stop the tears from building up. "I can't afford to stay here if we close. There are still expenses. Utilities. Even if I could find some sort of retail job, I was barely able to make rent on a studio doing that in D.C. Sure, the cost of living is lower here, but it's not going to stretch to this. So...that's it. She wins."

"I actually had an idea. It's...risky. Ish. But I could see it working." Emerson shifted in his seat.

"Let's hear it." It didn't seem likely that it would work, unless it involved magic lottery winnings. She fought a wince. That was unfair. And she was forgetting that God could make it work, if He chose to. That even sounded sulky in her head. *I'm sorry, Lord. I trust You. I do. But I might need a little extra help with it right now.*

"You bake bread every day, right?" Emerson leaned forward, his gaze locking on to Ruth's. "Would it be harder—especially if you had more time because you weren't caring for guests—to make some extra?"

She lifted a shoulder. "Not really. I might need a bigger mixer, or I could just do extra batches. Why?"

"In Seattle, Pam and I were members of a CSA and a CSB. They made our lives so much easier. Plus, we felt good about helping to support local families."

Corban squeezed Ruth's hand. "CSA I know. I've thought

about doing that myself. But I still do well enough on the wheat each year that it's easier to supplement with the farmers' market stall and not have to worry about memberships and so forth. But what's a CSB?"

"Community Supported Bakery instead of agriculture. In this case, bread. Who wouldn't love to get fresh bread once or twice a week? It beats the wrapper off the preservative laden nastiness they sell in the grocery store, and there are people who would want to participate simply because they're into local business. Throw in the fact that you're using local ingredients—"

"Not all of them. The wheat, sure. But it's not like I have an in with a local olive grove."

Emerson waved that away. "Sure, the fancy ingredients people will understand. But if the wheat is local, that's the biggie."

She nodded slowly. Her starter was completely based on wild yeast as well, so that was another bonus. Not that most people would care. But still. She pinched the bridge of her nose. She'd have to work out costs and see if it would actually have any sort of profit in a reasonable amount of time. She had a tiny bit in her bank account, but not enough to live on for long. A month maybe? "I guess it's possible. There are a lot of questions."

"I get that. Which is why I went ahead and contacted our CSB back in Seattle. They're happy to walk you through it, answer questions, that sort of thing. I have to say, they were so excited about the idea of another one forming I had to convince them not to just fly out to help set you up." Emerson grinned and pushed a piece of paper across the table toward Ruth. "Think about it. *Pray* about it. And as much as I'd like to say take all the time you need, I really think you're better off making a decision quickly. Because the sooner we can get Jaden off your case, the sooner you can decide if you want to reopen the B&B."

"Wait. What do you mean reopen? If I don't do this...if I decide to wait Jaden out and deal with it, why would I close? She can't win. You said that." Ruth glanced between Corban and Emerson. "Did I miss something?"

Emerson cringed. "Her attorney let on that they were working on a petition to have you closed down until the contest could be resolved. If you don't close voluntarily, I'm guessing you may end up shut down before the end of the month anyway."

"TALK TO ME." Corban slipped his arm around Ruth's shoulders when they returned to the lounge after walking Emerson to the door.

She sagged into the comfort and laid her head against his chest. "I don't know where to start."

"Top of your head?"

"Do people really want to buy homemade bread? It's so easy to make. Don't the people who want it just make their own?"

Corban laughed. "No. Take Pam. She's about as homemade and organic as it gets, but she's also a surgeon. You think she has time to make bread?"

That was a fair point. But for every Pam there had to be other people like Ruth who were content to do it themselves. "Bread's only two dollars. I can't compete with that."

"And I don't think people would expect you to. For home-made bread? I imagine people would pay six, maybe even seven dollars."

She goggled. "Seven dollars? You're insane. No one's going to pay that when they can go to the grocery store for less."

"They will once they taste your bread." Corban kissed her forehead. "I would. And I'm known for being cheap."

"You're just saying that because you're smitten with me."

"Not smitten. In love." He nudged her head off his chest and met her gaze. "I mean it."

She swallowed. There was no denying that he was in earnest. "I know you do. I...love you, too. I'm not sure what that means going forward, except that we both stand to get really hurt. But..."

"Shh." He lowered his lips to hers.

Ruth sighed and sank into the kiss. At least here she knew what she was doing. Even if nothing else in her life made sense, she had Corban. For now.

"WHAT'S ALL THIS?" Jonah peered over Ruth's shoulder at the papers she had spread out on the table in the kitchenette in her private rooms.

She sighed and pushed back her chair. As she walked to the mini-fridge to refill her glass with lemonade she filled her brother in on the conversation with Emerson and his idea for the CSB. "So I'm trying to figure out if it's even feasible. I mean, the idea is out there, as far as I'm concerned, but it would make a way for me to stay, at least for a while, if the money works."

"I think it's a fantastic idea." Jonah grabbed an apple out of the bowl on her counter and crunched into it. "Count me in. I haven't been able to find anything remotely interesting job-wise. And then, even once you reopen, I could keep on with the bread, if you'd help now and then."

"Seriously?" She hadn't considered that Jonah might be interested. "It's not fine dining. It's just bread."

"So? It's cooking. And it's good bread, too. Plus, there are so many options—if we devoted all our time to it? We could come up with some rocking options." Jonah drummed his fingers on the table. "We'd need a solid staple loaf, something for sandwiches. Maybe a second variety—oat based? I wonder if anyone grows oats locally. It'd be good to keep it all locally sourced. Then the fancier breads like you've already been playing with. Maybe a French loaf, too. Everyone loves a good baguette."

"You're serious." Ruth pulled the papers together into a pile. Were they really going to do this? She'd wanted to fulfill Naomi's wishes, to make her own dream of running an inn—or in this case, a B&B—come true. But if that was off the table, for now at least, baking bread was still something she loved.

"Heck yeah. This is awesome. When can we start?"

She opened her mouth, then snapped it shut. "I..."

"We need to call Micah and Malachi. They'll be jazzed. In fact, did you see Micah's text?"

Ruth shook her head. She'd put her cell phone...somewhere...after Corban left and hadn't bothered to go looking for it.

"He's pretty convinced he'll be out of work at the end of the week, and wanted to know if there's room for him here."

Her heart ached. Micah loved his job at the before and after school care center where he worked. It let him do a wide variety of things, from helping with homework to teaching kids to cook. He'd been bumping up against the director for months though, pretty much since she came on board, so this wasn't too surprising. The woman hadn't seemed to understand that men could want to be involved with kids, too, without having creepy hidden agendas. "I hope you told him yes. Especially with the B&B closed down for now, there's more than enough room."

"I did. But you should, too."

"What's Mal going to do out there all by himself?" Ruth chewed on her lower lip. He had a small network of friends and was plugged into a church, but he'd always been the most family-oriented of the four of them.

"Knowing Mal? Quit his job and move to Idaho to help us bake bread."

Ruth shook her head. She'd love that. Except that Mal was hopeless in the kitchen. But he was a business wiz. He'd probably have more than enough to keep him occupied. "Let me go find my cell and text Micah. Then you and I are going over these numbers to make sure this isn't the biggest mistake of my life."

14

"I'm so proud of you." Corban paused in the middle of arranging baskets of bread in the back of the stall. "You moved fast."

Ruth nodded, shifting a few loaves of bread she and Jonah had baked fresh that morning from one basket to another. "I figured it was better to dive in and see if it was feasible instead of wringing my hands. It helped that Jonah was all-in from pretty much the first mention."

Jonah hurried up with another basket and a file box. "Just finished chatting with Ms. Groves and we're set through the summer."

Ruth gulped. "The summer. I thought we were just giving this a trial..."

Jonah punched her shoulder. "Lighten up. If it doesn't fly, we'll talk to her again. As it is, I wanted to lock in our spot on Saturdays at the farmers' market. That way even if people don't want to sign up for weekly or bi-weekly bread through the CSB, they can grab a loaf while they're browsing."

She turned to Corban.

He raised his hands but couldn't stop the grin. When Jonah

glommed onto an idea, he apparently ran with it. "I had nothing to do with it other than pointing out Ms. Groves. But, for the record, I think it's a good idea. Even when I'm here selling, I end up purchasing from the other vendors. Never underestimate the power of an impulse buy. Especially if you're giving out samples."

Ruth nodded. "I need to set that up next. You've got the paperwork for the sign-ups?"

Jonah lifted the file box. "In here. Though we really ought to get a laptop."

"One thing at a time, okay? For now, we can translate paper into the computer when we get home. I can't imagine it's going to take all that long. How many people could possibly want to join?"

Corban stepped back and admired his handiwork. "There you go. That looks pretty nice, and, if I'm not wrong, here comes your first member. Hey, Pam!"

Pam hurried to the table, her pocketbook swinging madly at her side. "Is what Emerson said true? You're really starting a CSB?"

"That's the plan." Ruth sounded skeptical.

Jonah nudged her out of the way with a grin. "Hi, I'm Jonah Baxter, Ruth's brother. And yes, we are. Can I show you our membership options?"

Pam nodded and reached for the packet of paper Jonah offered. He talked her through the options, answering questions as they arose, and was collecting a check and signed form before too much time had passed.

Corban slid his arm around Ruth's waist and leaned down to whisper in her ear. "He's got skills."

She nodded.

"Still think it's a bad idea?" Corban searched Ruth's face. He didn't want her to do something she wasn't excited about, or that she thought was dumb. But he also didn't want her to feel cornered, like she had no options. She'd run back to D.C. Or somewhere else. And he needed her to stay here. To stay with him.

Ruth blew out a breath. "Since Jonah's well on his way to enrolling a second customer and there's a little bit of a line forming, I guess not. Which means, I suppose, that you need to get out of my way. I need to put on my saleswoman face and offer these people some samples."

She turned, collecting the board that held half-slices of various bread types. Pausing, she brushed her lips across Corban's. "Thank you."

He winked. "My pleasure."

"You have time for lunch?" Ruth offered a tired smile from the doorway of the barn.

Corban wiped his hands on a rag and stretched his back. "I could eat. Is it really lunchtime already?"

"Nearly one."

He frowned at the tractor. He'd wasted half a day fixing it and wasn't positive it was going to hold. He'd probably have been better off calling the mechanic, but Dad had drummed into him that you took a look at it yourself before spending money. Over the years, he'd become a pretty competent mechanic, at least on his own equipment. He wasn't looking to go into business for other people. "I should wash up. Want to eat in the kitchen?"

"It's a pretty day. I thought maybe we could eat outside?"

He shrugged. He wasn't really set up for picnics, but there was a little patch of grass out front. "All right. I'll find you in a few."

He patted his leg for Spock and angled across the back yard to the house. Maybe washing his hands would let him scrape off some of the mood that had been plaguing him since Saturday, too. Four days was long enough for brooding. Especially when he couldn't put his finger on the problem.

When he was cleaned up, he stepped out on the front porch and stopped. She was a picture. She'd spread out a blanket on the little patch of grass under the oak tree and was sitting with her legs tucked under her. Spock had found her and curled up at her side. A fist grabbed his heart. He wanted this.

"There you are." Ruth beamed at him and patted the blanket. "You need a picnic table."

He nodded. "I guess I do. Mom always talked about getting something, but she never could decide on a set. Same thing happened when they moved to Florida. They had an amazing lanai and only a couple of folding chairs—you know the cheap ones you get at any discount store? Dad said he didn't care. Probably didn't."

Ruth waited until he'd lowered himself to the ground before she opened the basket. "I made sandwiches. I hope that's okay. It's not fancy."

"I don't need fancy." He grabbed her hand and brought it to his lips.

She beamed before continuing to set out lunch. "I never thought I'd say it, but I'm a little tired of baking bread."

"Already?" That wasn't good. Who knew how long she'd have to keep it up if she was going to stay in the area? "Any word from Emerson?"

She shook her head. "It's only been a couple of days. I can imagine Jaden watching and waiting to see if I'm serious before giving up. At least Emerson said her attorney is aware now, and probably less likely to do anything without all the facts in place first. And then, if he has the facts, there won't be anything to do anyway. Waiting is horrible."

"I can imagine. Waiting is kind of the mainstay of farming though, so I guess you get used to it. You put the seeds in and then you have to wait and see what grows. You can only control so much. After that, you have to leave it to God."

Ruth sighed. "A lot like life. I'm working on it. At least we had a good turnout on Saturday. Twenty signups was about nineteen more than I anticipated. And we've had a handful via phone so far this week, plus some one off orders. Folks who liked the samples but came back to buy after we sold out. It just might work. Jonah has all these ideas."

Corban chuckled. He could imagine. Jonah seemed like a take it and run guy. "Like what?"

"He's off looking at a space in the Arcadia Shopping Center."

"A storefront?"

She nodded. "Like I said, he has ideas. And with Micah coming out, and Malachi too, if I know my brothers, well, it could turn into a family business."

"Not on main? Downtown?"

Ruth shook her head. "Jonah didn't want to compete, even tangentially, with Demi's Delights."

"Sounds reasonable. What about expenses?" Corban reached for a sandwich, then paused and took Ruth's hand. "Hold that thought, let's bless the meal."

He bowed his head and offered a prayer of thanksgiving for the food and blessing for Ruth and her brothers.

"Amen." Ruth unwrapped her sandwich. "He's worried that Jaden will see us based out of the house and keep up her contest of the will, even though it's totally different than the B&B. I can see her using just that sort of twisted logic. I'm not sold, but he's looked into some small business loans and I guess thinks the risk is worth the benefit."

"Hmm. This hits the spot, thanks." Corban patted her knee. He didn't like taking loans. He'd done it in the past, but then every move he'd made had been focused on paying it back as quickly as he could. It's one of the reasons he was still nursing the old tractor along. It'd be good to get a newer one, but not until he'd saved up the price. Maybe next year, if things went well this season. On the other hand, it wasn't his place to object. Not really.

"We'll wait until Micah gets here before we do anything permanent. He should be here tomorrow. He left Sunday, but I know he wanted to stop and see a few things along the way, if only to break up the thirty-four-hour drive." Ruth dipped her hand into a container and emerged with a slice of apple. "But as it is, we've baked more than thirty loaves of bread each day so far this week and all but a couple have sold. And while it'll need to pick up if it's going to become sustainable, it's a good start."

His eyebrows winged up. "That's great."

She nodded. "Thus the storefront idea. It's inconvenient for people to come to the house just to get a loaf or two of bread. And even though there's another bakery in town, it's not really the same since it's tied to a cafe and is focused on Greek desserts. There's the grocery store, of course, but..."

"Not really the same. I'm glad this is working out so well. And that your other brothers are joining you. I know you missed them."

"I did. But not enough to ask them to leave if they were settled. Micah leaving his job is nothing sort of a miracle. Malachi is a little easier to understand, though he hasn't confirmed yet. But we've always been close. I know the distance has been eating at him."

"Mostly I'm glad you're staying. For purely selfish reasons." Corban balled up the wrapper from his sandwich and tossed it back into the basket. "Do you have time for a walk? I wanted to check on the lettuce fields. They should be ready to harvest in two weeks or so, once we're into June. That's when I'll start my own booth at the market."

"I've got time." Ruth stood and wrapped her arms around his waist, tipping her head back. "Especially if you offered a kiss or two as incentive."

Corban chuckled and lowered his lips to meet hers. "That I can do."

15

Ruth closed the oven door and looked around the commercial kitchen. The shopping-center space had been a good idea, especially since they'd been able to find a unit that was already mostly fitted out for what they needed. It had only taken a week to make the changes they'd needed and now, three weeks later, Micah was here and they were up and running. Business was good. People continued to sign up for the CSB—who knew so many people would choose fresh bread given the option? And when they stopped in to pick up their orders, they inevitably grabbed one of the fancy loaves as well.

"I hate to say it, but you were right." Ruth smiled at Jonah as he came in the back door with a box of ingredients.

He grinned. "Anything from Emerson? I know this isn't your dream and having the B&B closed for a month isn't what you wanted."

"Nothing yet. But he's hopeful that we'll have resolution soon." She frowned as fire trucks screamed past the shopping center headed south toward the outskirts of town. "Gosh, I hope that's not anyone we know."

"Could be a false alarm. That happens." Micah pushed open the swinging door that separated the kitchen from the customer area. "How are the sourdough loaves coming? We're nearly out."

"Just put them in the oven." Ruth checked the clock. "But it's nearly noon. Things taper off until what, three?"

"About that, yeah, when people start thinking about dinner. You in a rush to go somewhere?"

Ruth laughed. "Mal should be getting here soon. He was only about four hours out last night when he stopped. I wanted to be there to welcome him."

"Go. We've got this." Micah made a shooing motion. "But bring him by as soon as he's settled."

"We'll see. Tomorrow's soon enough. I might not be back, depending on how he's feeling."

"Or if Corban finished up whatever harvest he's working on today."

Heat flooded her cheeks at Jonah's words. "Just remember, Micah, that only Jonah gets to wait on the girl who comes by every other day at precisely three o'clock."

Micah snickered.

Jonah spluttered.

Ruth waved. At least she'd managed to get the last word. And the girl really was quite pretty. It'd be nice to see her brothers settled. Especially since she and Corban had been talking more and more about the future. Marriage. Kids. She wanted those things with him. For the first time in her life, she was ready to jump in with both feet.

A plume of black smoke caught her eye as she turned toward the B&B. Her heart started racing. Her foot fell heavier on the accelerator. It couldn't be. *Please, God, don't let it be.*

"No. No, no, no, no!" She threw the car into park at the foot of the driveway, behind a fire truck and jumped out of the car.

"Miss? You need to stop. Miss! You can't go in there." A burly fireman in his yellow suit grabbed her arm.

"This is my house. My inn. I have to get inside." Ruth scanned the building for any sign of flames. Not seeing any, she shook her arm, trying to dislodge his grip.

"Did you have any guests?"

"No. No one's there. Except—oh no. Malachi. My brother was getting into town. I told him where I hid the key and that he should just go in. Mal!" She shouted, even though it was pointless. He couldn't hear.

"That sounds like the young man who called it in. He's over here. Let me take you to him." The fireman guided Ruth back down the driveway and across the road where Malachi stood with Corban.

Ruth ran to her brother and wrapped her arms around him, breathing out a quiet prayer of thanks that he was okay. She stepped back and signed as she talked. "You made it. And saw the fire? You weren't inside? You're okay?"

He smiled and grabbed her hands, squeezed, and let go so he could sign. "I'm okay. I was just pulling in when I saw the smoke. I called 9-1-1."

"Thank you." Ruth turned to Corban. "How did you know?"

"I heard the trucks and came to see what was going on before I called you. They got here fast."

A shout went up across the road as a fireman exited the front door with someone in his arms. Who was that? She glanced at Corban and Malachi again before hurrying back across the road.

She jogged over to where the firefighter had set the woman on the bumper of the truck. She had an oxygen mask strapped to her face and a blanket around her shoulders, but there was no mistaking her.

"Jaden? What are you doing here?"

"Ma'am, I thought we asked you to stay across the road."

Ruth crossed her arms and glared at the fireman. "This woman had no business being in my house."

Jaden pulled the mask off. "Not yours. It's mine."

"You know very well you have practically no chance of succeeding in a contest of the will. I know your attorney has told you that, because he's told me that he told you. What is wrong with you?"

Something flickered in Jaden's eyes. "Maybe neither of us should have it."

Ruth's mouth fell open. "You did this."

"Prove it." Coughs racked Jaden's body and the fireman pushed the mask back over her face.

"You need to get an arson investigator out here. I want her arrested."

The man sighed. "Ma'am, we've sent to Twin Falls, but we don't have someone in town who does that. That said, it was obvious the fire was set deliberately. She needs to be in a hospital. As soon as the ambulance gets here, that's where she's headed. Can you *please* go back across the road, and stay there, until we're finished?"

Tears filled Ruth's eyes but she nodded. "Can you at least tell me how bad it is?"

"It's just the back rooms, looked like a separate suite of some sort. There might be a little smoke damage, but it shouldn't be too hard to get squared away once you get the all clear." He pointed across the road.

She gave Jaden one more sour look before trudging back to Corban and her brother. Of course it was her private rooms. She'd stopped locking them when she'd stopped taking guests. That must've thrilled Jaden, to be able to strike at the heart of where Ruth lived.

"I called Emerson. He's going to call that woman's attorney

and the cops. This is ridiculous." Corban put an arm around Ruth's shoulders and hugged her close. "I'm so sorry."

"Why does she hate me so much?" She buried her head into his chest.

Malachi touched her shoulder.

She looked at her brother. Thank God he hadn't been hurt.

His hands flashed as he answered the question she hadn't realized she'd asked aloud. "She wanted what you had with her sister and never understood that she already did, until she let jealousy get in the way."

RUTH DRAGGED another trash bag out to the curb and turned to look at the house. The police and fire inspector had been in and out all morning and finally cleared her to go in after lunch. She just wanted to get things back to normal as fast as she could. But the bread still needed to get baked and the vegetables harvested, which was why she'd shooed Corban back to his fields and her brothers to the shop. She was perfectly capable of throwing things away.

A car beeped as it turned into the driveway. She frowned. Now what?

Emerson climbed out, opened the back door so the boys could get out, and waved. "Go play. Stay where I can see you."

The boys whooped and ran into the yard.

"How bad is it?"

Ruth shrugged. "I don't have a lot of experience to compare with, but it's really just the kitchen and living room in my suite at the back. It doesn't look like it lasted long enough for there to be smoke damage, and apparently she tripped and hit her head before she could set any more fires. So it could be worse."

Emerson nodded. "She's admitted it."

"Seriously?"

"Yep. Just got a call from her former attorney, who is incredibly unhappy to have taken her on as a client and is cutting ties as fast as he can. My understanding is that she'll probably plead out."

"I don't care. I just want her out of my life."

"I'm pretty sure that's a done deal. Once you get everything cleaned up, I'd say you're fine to go ahead and start taking guests again. After this incident, the slim chance she had at overturning the will is gone."

Ruth let out a breath. That was something, at least. "Thanks, Emerson."

"Not a problem. Let me know if you need anything else, okay? Pam's over the moon about the bread, as are the boys. Oh, hey, do you ever do muffins?"

"Muffins? No."

Emerson frowned. "Well, maybe it's something to consider."

"Sure. I'll mention it to Jonah."

Emerson called to the boys who only needed a little cajoling to get back in the car. She lifted a hand as he backed out of the driveway. Muffins. Took all kinds. She trudged inside and detoured upstairs. If she was back in business, she should make sure the guest rooms were ready and worry about her own space later.

16

Corban hid the bouquet of sunflowers he'd picked up at Blossoms by the Akers when he'd been down at the garden center for some plants yesterday. He knocked on the kitchen door of the once again fully-functional B&B. As soon as she'd started taking reservations last week, Ruth had received three bookings. They'd arrived at the start of the week-end. One couple had even joined Ruth at church before heading out to explore.

Ruth pulled open the door with a grin. "Hey. I'm sorry I couldn't do lunch. With guests and everything, I needed to get back and tidy up a little."

"It's okay. Where are the guys?"

"Napping. All three of them. I guess getting up before the sun six days a week to bake does a number on you." She grinned. "Come on in."

He whipped the flowers around with a flourish. "I was hoping you might want to go for a walk with me."

"Oh, these are lovely." Ruth buried her nose in the flowers, then sneezed. "I forget sunflowers don't smell great. But they're so cheery. Let me put them in water and get some shoes."

Corban tucked his hands in his pockets as she hurried out of the kitchen, his fingers closing around the small, velvet box that held his mother's engagement ring. His stomach jittered. Was it too soon? Not in terms of their relationship, but was there already too much upheaval in her life? Jaden, her brothers, the CSB...even the harvest, in some ways, was a change, since it had taken up lots of his previously free time during the day. He'd come by most evenings still, and they'd talked or played a game together. Or spent time kissing on the couch.

He smiled.

"What's that for?" Ruth came back without the flowers and with sneakers on her feet.

"I love you." He reached out and took her hand.

"I love you, too." She breathed in deeply. "This is just what I needed."

"What is?"

"Time alone with you." She cocked her head to the side and smiled. "And probably the fresh air."

Corban squeezed her hand as they crossed the road and wove through the fields. Periodically Ruth would ask what one thing or another was. It was good she had interest in the farm. It was a part of him. Would she mind living in the farmhouse and running the B&B from there? His mother had never seen it as a problem, and it would free up the main floor suite as well. Though maybe her brothers would want to live there. These were all details. He was getting ahead of himself.

"You're quiet."

"Sorry." He flashed a grin. "We're almost there."

"I don't think I've ever been over this way." She craned her neck around as they walked.

"Here we are." He pushed open a white picket gate and held it as she walked through. "This was my mother's garden. She used to spend hours out here while Dad was in the fields. In the evening, they'd come sit by the pond and listen to the fountain. I let it go for a while after they moved away. It always seemed like I was trespassing on their private space. But then came you."

Ruth's eyes grew wide. "This is beautiful."

He watched as she moved from his mother's rose bushes that formed a sort of wall around the space to the beds he'd planted with multi-colored flowers. When she came to the small pond with water trickling down stair-stepped rocks she stopped and turned to him. "I see why they came out here. It's like a little piece of heaven."

Corban crossed the garden and took her hand again as he lowered to the wrought iron bench facing the water.

Ruth sat beside him and sighed. "Thank you for bringing me here."

He shifted, turning so he was facing her, his gaze locked with hers. "I'm hoping this can become our spot. A place we come to remember the beauty and romance of love, even on the days when things are harder than it seems like they should be. My parents had a long marriage, a good one, but it wasn't perfect. They argued and they made up. And they never stopped loving one another." Corban slid off the bench onto one knee and fished the box out of his pocket. "I want that with you, if you'll have me."

Ruth's eyes filled with tears. She blinked, but one escaped trickling down her cheek. "Oh, Corban. I want that, too."

Heart thundering in his chest, he opened the box to reveal the simple solitaire in a plain gold band. "This was my mother's. It served her well and I know she'd be thrilled for you to wear it. Will you marry me?"

She reached for the ring, eyes glistening with tears, and slipped it on her finger before gathering him into her arms. "Yes. Oh absolutely yes."

His lips found hers and the sounds of the bubbling water faded as he lost himself in their future.

PREVIEW OF MUFFINS & MOONBEAMS

Ready for more? Here's a preview of Muffins & Moonbeams, the first full-length book in the Baxter Family Bakery series.

Malachi Baxter pushed a hand through his hair and scowled at the computer screen. He hadn't built a website since high school. How did he get stuck with this job? Oh, right. Business degree. Which meant handling the finances and such, but the website? He scooted away from the machine and stood. He needed to talk to his brothers.

He stepped out of the tiny office at the back of the bakery and into a wall of heat. His oldest brother, Jonah, was measuring ingredients into a huge mixing bowl. His lips were moving, but with his brother's face half-turned Malachi couldn't quite lip read well enough to make out the words. Was he singing? He touched Jonah's shoulder.

"Hey, Mal. Done with the website already?" Jonah set the measuring cup aside and dusted his hands on the apron tied around his waist. "That was fast."

Malachi shook his head and signed. "We need to hire someone. It's an investment that'll pay off in the long run. If I do it, it's going to look like someone's ten year old put it together over the weekend."

Jonah laughed. "That bad?"

Malachi nodded. He'd drag his brothers back to see what he'd been playing with all morning if they insisted, but it was embarrassing.

"All right. Let's check with Micah, but if you say we need it and can afford it, then I'm game." Jonah strode across the kitchen to the swinging door that led to the front of the bakery where Micah manned the counter.

Malachi sighed and followed.

Micah handed change and a bag of bread to one of their regulars—Malachi searched his memory for the name and came up blank—and turned when the light above the door that served as the hearing impaired version of a doorbell flashed and the customer left. "Uh oh. If Mal's out of the office, something must be up."

Malachi clutched his stomach and feigned laughter before sticking his tongue out.

Jonah shook his head. "Nothing serious. Mal thinks we should hire the website out."

"Rusty?" Micah raised his eyebrows.

Malachi signed, not bothering to speak along with it since they were alone in the bakery. "When was the last time you did a website?"

"Fair enough. Works for me. You notice I didn't volunteer to do any of that stuff, right?" Micah squatted and collected a towel from under the counter. He ran the cloth over the display case, scrubbing at some imagined spot. "Do what you think is best."

Jonah nodded. "Agreed. And since you're handling all the

business end, I don't really care about details. You've got a good head on your shoulders and won't dig us into debt."

It was good his brothers had faith in him. Someone needed to. He nodded and eased back through the door into the kitchen. No point in hanging around out where customers came to gawk at the deaf man. In D.C. he hadn't been a novelty. There were all sorts of people in the greater metropolitan area that made up what had been home his whole life. And mostly people didn't bother staring at the ones who were different. In Arcadia Valley different stuck out. Oh, they were nice about it. Malachi doubted anyone genuinely had any motive other than learning about something they didn't encounter every day. But that didn't keep him from feeling like a circus sideshow because he couldn't hear. He hadn't felt that way since right after the accident that cost him his hearing when he was young.

Back in the office, he pushed the door mostly shut, a signal that he was involved and shouldn't be disturbed if at all possible. A quick search online revealed what he suspected, there were more web designers in the world than made sense. How did he sort out the bad ones and find the good? Malachi drummed his fingers on the desk and reached for his cell phone to tap out a quick text to his sister, Ruth. The B&B had a nice site with a lot of the same kinds of functionality that they'd need. He set his cell back in the charging cradle that flashed brightly when his phone vibrated and turned to the computer. It was mid-morning. Ruth was probably cleaning rooms and wouldn't get to her phone for a while. But there was no rush.

With a glance toward the door and only the barest twinge of guilt, Malachi started up Orion's Quest and logged in. There weren't many players online in the middle of the morning, but there were always folks in other time zones, or people, like him, sneaking in a battle during a slow time at work. He skimmed the activity log. No one he played with was on, but he'd been storing up solo missions. Maybe he could knock one of them out. If his ship was repaired. He'd parked it in a dry dock when he logged out the night before, there should have been enough time for the fixes to be finished. And if not, he'd wander this outpost—where was he again? Didn't matter, really. Some new outpost on the edge of civilized space, getting ready to head into the frontier and see where his fortune lay. Before that, he could use an armor upgrade. Maybe some new weapons. If he had the cash after he paid for repairs.

The chat bar at the bottom of his screen notified him that Scarlet Fire had logged in. His heart sped up and he grinned as he opened up a direct message box.

"What are you doing on in the middle of the morning? Don't you have work?"

"Ha ha. I could ask you the same thing. Slow day?"

Malachi glanced at his cell phone cradle before typing again. "Waiting on a text. Thought I'd check on my ship, maybe start a quest."

"Need a first mate?"

Colorful lights flashed in the corner of his eye. Of course. He sighed and grabbed the phone. Sure enough, Ruth had come through with the contact info for her web designer. "Never mind. Gotta run. You'll be on tonight?"

"Of course. See you then."

Malachi took two minutes to run down and spring his ship from the repair facility. At least that way when he did have time to play he'd be ready to go. With a final check that he'd set himself to be able to scoot out on a mission as soon as he logged back in, he exited the game and opened a web browser. He liked the website for the Fairview, but there was nothing wrong with checking out other references just to be sure before making contact.

Want a Free Book?

If you enjoyed *Loaves and Wishes* and would like to read more of my work, you can get a book simply by signing up for my newsletter here: http://bit.ly/2goAGvf

Author's Note

Thank you for reading *Loaves & Wishes!* I hope that you enjoyed it! I would appreciate it if you'd help others enjoy it too by leaving a review on Amazon, Goodreads, and any other retail site you frequent. Word of mouth is how most people say they find new books to read, so I'd love it if you'd also consider telling your friends about it. Any success my books have is owed to readers like you who take the time to tell others about my stories. Thank you, from the bottom of my heart.

I had so much fun being part of the Arcadia Valley series. Now that all six authors have completed their series and we've separated back out into individual projects, I find myself missing the conversations we had in our little author group about where a building should be or what might be happening in town during a particular month. The Baxter Family Bakery series can be read as a standalone series, but I hope you'll look for the other books that were originally part of the Arcadia Valley series and spend some more time in town when you're finished.

You can always keep up to date with my writing news via my newsletter. There's a sign-up form at my website http://bit.ly/2goAGvf and also on my author Facebook page http://www.Facebook.com/ElizabethMaddrey.

I continue to owe a huge debt of gratitude to my husband and sons for giving me the time to write, my sister for her unflinching support and encouragement, and my critique partners Lynellen Perry, Heather Gray and Jan Elder for catching all the times I use the same word six times in two paragraphs.

More than anything, I'm grateful that God continues to give me words and makes it possible for me to write them down.

I'd love to hear from you! You can connect with me on Facebook my webpage or via email.

ABOUT THE AUTHOR

Elizabeth Maddrey is a semi-reformed computer geek and homeschooling mother of two who lives in the suburbs of Washington D.C. When she isn't writing, Elizabeth is a voracious consumer of books. She loves to write about Christians who struggle through their lives, dealing with sin and receiving God's grace on their way to their own romantic happily ever after.

facebook.com/ElizabethMaddrey

instagram.com/elizabethmaddrey

amazon.com/author/ElizabethMaddrey

bookbub.com/authors/elizabeth-maddrey

ALSO BY ELIZABETH MADDREY

Hope Ranch Series

Hope for Christmas

Peacock Hill Romance Series

A Heart Restored

A Heart Reclaimed

A Heart Realigned

Arcadia Valley Romance – Baxter Family Bakery Series

Loaves & Wishes

Muffins & Moonbeams

Cookies & Candlelight

Donuts & Daydreams

The 'Operation Romance' Series

Operation Mistletoe

Operation Valentine

Operation Fireworks

Operation Back-to-School

The 'Taste of Romance' Series

A Splash of Substance

A Pinch of Promise

A Dash of Daring

A Handful of Hope

A Tidbit of Trust

The 'Grant Us Grace' Series

Joint Venture

Wisdom to Know

Courage to Change

Serenity to Accept

Pathway to Peace

The 'Remnants' Series:

Faith Departed

Hope Deferred

Love Defined

Stand alone novellas

Kinsale Kisses: An Irish Romance

Luna Rosa (part of A Tuscan Legacy)

Non-Fiction

A Walk in the Valley: Christian encouragement for your journey
through infertility

For the most recent listing of all my books, please visit my website.